WHERE THE HEART IS

Lissa decides she has something to prove and takes a job as a housekeeper. However, with her privileged background, she's ill prepared for such work and all too often finds herself in danger of her true identity being discovered. Fortunately her boss, the gorgeous Dom, sees her other talents. He soon realises that it wasn't just a housekeeper he needed to make his life complete. But when has the course of true love ever run smoothly?

CHRISSIE LOVEDAY

WHERE THE HEART IS

Complete and Unabridged

LINFORD
Leicester

First published in Great Britain in 2010

First Linford Edition
published 2011

Copyright © 2010 by Chrissie Loveday

British Library CIP Data

Loveday, Chrissie.
  Where the heart is. - -
(Linford romance library)
  1. Housekeepers- -Fiction. 2. Love stories.
  3. Large type books.
  I. Title II. Series
  823.9′2–dc22

  ISBN 978–1–44480–605–2

Published by
F. A. Thorpe (Publishing)
Anstey, Leicestershire

Set by Words & Graphics Ltd.
Anstey, Leicestershire
Printed and bound in Great Britain by
T. J. International Ltd., Padstow, Cornwall

This book is printed on acid-free paper

'You're A Very Wealthy Girl'

'You don't really seem to be quite my usual type of lady,' the woman in the employment agency told Lissa. 'And as for your qualifications, well, they do leave you something short.'

'I did follow a Cordon Bleu cookery course.'

'Well yes, but there's more to the job than simply being a good cook. Do you know about housekeeping? Organising other staff?'

Lissa crossed her fingers and fibbed gently.

'Of course. I do have experience of running quite a large establishment. Look, perhaps I'm wasting your time. I'm sorry. It was a foolish idea.'

She collected her leather shoulder bag from the floor next to her seat and

1

managed to tip it the wrong way. The expensive contents showered down.

Gold Gucci pen, soft leather wallet, gold chain she'd pushed down into the depths one day and forgotten about, top of the range mobile phone, a bottle of her favourite perfume . . . the lot. She scooped it up and began to apologise again. Her possessions hardly looked like those of someone looking for a job in a small town employment agency. She coloured slightly, realising she had made a stupid mistake. How could she have thought she might carry it off? She cursed her father under her breath for pushing her into this charade.

'Just a moment, Melissa,' her austere interviewer said. 'Please sit down.' Lissa stared and sat back on the uncomfortable chair. 'I make no promises but there is a possible opportunity you might try. It's purely temporary, you understand. If, and I stress if Mr Wetherill agrees, you might assume the role of Cook/Housekeeper for him for a while. He will need to meet you first of course and if you think you could manage to hold yourself together, you may just do.'

'And precisely who is Mr Wetherill?' Her brain was whirring. The name sounded slightly familiar. Perhaps he was something exciting in the music world or TV.

'One of our clients. He owns several properties but needs someone at his Buckinghamshire home for a short time. You may know it, as you are familiar with the area. Templars Mansion?'

She had indeed heard of it. More than that, she had actually visited the place with her father, some years ago. Would she be able to carry off her current ploy?

As far as she could remember, Mr Wetherill must be well over seventy by now. He would never remember the gawky schoolgirl who had once sulked in a corner while he and her father had conducted their business. Old books.

They were both fanatics of old books.

She had a vague memory of a dog. A spaniel. It was the one saving grace of the place, an over-furnished, dark-panelled place, stuffed with antiques. Did she even want to visit the mansion?

She was about to turn it down when she remembered her father's last words to her before she had stormed out. It almost brought tears to her eyes. How could he have been so cruel?

How could she have been so awful back? They had always meant the world to each other.

'I'll certainly go to meet the . . . gentleman,' she said meekly and totally out of her usual character.

'Very well. Wait in the reception area please, while I make a few phone calls. I shall of course have to contact your previous employer, before I can recommend you to Mr Wetherill.'

Lissa left the room, again crossing her fingers. She hoped that dear old Batesy would carry it off. He had been part of their home for as long as she could remember, doing just about everything except the cooking which he conceded to his wife.

Lissa and Bates held each other in mutual fondness and he would do anything for her, she knew. She had arranged for him to provide a reference, should she need it.

A few minutes later, the elegant owner of the agency called her back, passing a neatly written card with the agency's heading at the top.

'Mr Wetherill will see you at two this afternoon. He may require you to work immediately.'

'Thank you,' Lissa said gratefully. 'Thank you very much. I take it you contacted Mr Bates?'

'Indeed. He gave a most glowing account of you. I may have had my doubts but he convinced me to give you this opportunity. He was slightly unforthcoming about the real reason you wished to leave your post.'

I bet he was, Lissa grinned to herself. She would show her father who was a spoiled brat who could never get a job. She shuddered at the memory of the dreadful row they'd had.

Desperate to assert herself, she'd gone to a local restaurant with Tony Mason, a young man who worked at the local garage. Her father had arrived home at the same moment as she was getting off the back of Tony's motorbike.

Alistair Langham had exploded with anger and ordered her into the house. Tony had left, looking slightly bewildered and she had seen nothing of him since.

'How could you, Daddy? I'm not a child. Tony was good fun and we had a nice evening together. I'll never be able to hold my head up again,' she shouted at her father in the imposing hallway of their home.

'Don't you realise your position? You're a very wealthy girl or will be. You've never had to think beyond your next ballgown. Of course anyone from hereabouts will want to take you out.

They'd all like a slice of our money . . . our lifestyle.'

'I just want to be like any normal girl. Go out and have some fun occasionally.'

'Oh yes? And who from around here can keep you in the way you're used to?'

'I could get a job.'

He stared at her with scorn dripping out of every pore. The two pairs of green eyes glared at each other, so alike. Father and daughter were equally stubborn and neither was giving an inch.

'You? Get a job. Don't make me laugh. You haven't a clue, have you? Every male in the district wants you for your money. Where on earth do you keep your brains? I think there must be a lot of empty air between your ears. You're behaving like an empty headed waste of space. Thoroughly spoiled.'

Lissa stepped away from him. Shocked to the core. How dare he say something so dreadful.

'Daddy . . . ' she whispered in shock. 'You're so wound up in your own world, you don't even know me any more.' She turned away and ran up to her room.

'Lissa . . . I'm sorry. Come back. I shouldn't have spoken like that.' He followed her upstairs and knocked on the door. 'Lissa. Please. Open your door. I have to go away in the morning. I don't want us to part like this. I was just so very angry. You're a very special person . . . You're my whole life.'

But the door remained closed as Lissa simmered inside her room. It was a luxurious room which had gradually evolved from the childish room of the little girl to a well-designed adult room. Feminine but uncluttered.

She'd show her father. She'd get a job and prove she could do something worthwhile. Now here she was, a possible housekeeper for someone.

★　★　★

Two hours later, she made her way up the long, imposing drive to Templars. It was an old, redbrick building, dating back to the eighteenth century. It was certainly a beautiful house but more like a museum than a home.

She parked her borrowed car outside. Thinking her own sporty model didn't look quite right for the role she was hoping to play, Bates had lent her his own small saloon. She left her keys for him to use but he vowed he would never dare to drive hers in exchange. She rang the bell feeling rather nervous. This really was something new for her and she so wanted to make it work.

'Miss Langham? Mr Wetherill is expecting you.' The young girl, presumably some sort of maid opened the door and showed her into what was obviously a library of sorts. Many of the shelves were empty and there were several boxes of books on the floor. With slight hesitation, she stepped towards the youngish man sitting at the table.

'I'm here to see Mr Wetherill,' she said nervously. The man before her was very attractive and not at all what she was expecting.

'You are seeing him. Dominic Wetherill. Dom to most folks. Pleased to meet you, Miss Langham.'

'Lissa. Melissa really, but known to everyone as Lissa. But I thought Mr Wetherill was . . . well, older.'

'You must be thinking of my father. Sadly, he died a few weeks ago. I am now desperately trying to sort out his estate.'

'I'm so sorry,' Lissa replied. 'I didn't realise.'

She looked at her potential employer. He must be around thirty, she decided. All this, she thought as she glanced at the room and good looks as well. His hair was as dark as soot and the azure blue eyes would have made an impact on any female, let alone one who was sorely in need of some comfort at this moment in time.

'I understand you're looking for a

cook housekeeper on a temporary basis. I have a Cordon Bleu Certificate from the . . . '

'Oh I'm sure you'll do fine. If Lettie Jenkins recommends you, I have every confidence. Do you know anything about books?'

'Books?' she echoed. 'A bit. Pages, covers. Words. That sort of thing?' She deliberately talked herself down. If she let on too much at this stage, she was hardly going to appear a credible housekeeper.

She actually knew a great deal about books. She should do. It was her father's passion in life. When he wasn't doing his mega deals around the world, he adored trading in rare books. All too often he couldn't bear to part with them and they ended up as yet more items in his own collection. In fact, come to think of it, that was the reason for their visit to Templars, all those years ago.

'I have to sell some of them. Inheritance taxes . . . you know the sort

11

of thing. I suspect I might have to sell this place eventually. It will be a devastating blow when it comes to it, but I suppose one shouldn't try to keep a museum going when all you need is a home. Besides, I doubt I shall be here very much of the time. I'm sorry. You'll want to see your room and someone needs to tell you what's wanted in the way of duties.

'Jane will know some of it. Just do your own thing, otherwise. There will be various guests coming over the next few days. There's a calendar somewhere with all the details.'

He went back to studying the books and she turned to leave the room. He seemed uninterested in everything apart from the books, she decided. This was possibly about to become a rather boring experience. All the same, she must do it, just to prove to her father that she wasn't the spoiled, brainless little fool he'd accused her of being. And what had he got against Tony Mason, anyway? She shuddered as she remembered her father's hateful words. How could he have said such awful things?

'Jane?' she called softly. A baize door opened and the girl who'd let her in appeared from what must be the kitchen.

'Hi. Lissa,' she said holding out her hand. Shyly the girl took it and lowered her eyes, blushing. 'How do you do? I thought you'd be well, older. After Elsie left, I expected someone more like her.'

'Officially, I'm just a temp. I gather things have been changing quite a bit around here?'

'Certainly have. Since the old Mr Wetherill went, we've been working flat out to try to get straight. I think the young Mr Wetherill is planning to sell up. When Elsie heard the rumour, she decided it was time to retire. I'll show you round.'

The girl chatted as she led Lissa from room to room, explaining roughly what they had been used for. Lissa was delighted to see the kitchen looked clean and modern, unlike the rest of the house.

'Are there any animals?' she asked suddenly, remembering the spaniel.

'Not since the old dog died. That must be about eight years ago. Just after I came here as a junior. Now, let's go and look upstairs. You can have a choice of two or even three rooms. I don't expect Mr Wetherill will care much where you go.'

Keeping a house of this size in any decent condition was clearly going to be a lot of work. Much to her relief, Lissa discovered that there was a woman who came in daily to do the heavy cleaning and a gardener who appeared as often as he thought fit, usually three or four days a week.

He was supposed to be full-time, but evidently had some problems in getting to work every day. No-one had dared challenge him for several years. But, the gardens looked immaculate, so nobody complained.

'Jane,' called a voice from downstairs.

14

'Jane? Where are you? I need some help.'

'I'd better go. Mr Wetherill gets a bit bad tempered sometimes. I don't think he means any harm but I'm a bit scared of him, to tell you the truth. Him being so young and well, good looking.'

'It's OK, I'll go,' Lissa offered. 'I need to get to know him and see what he expects of me.' She skipped down the wide staircase and into the library. 'Will I do?' she asked.

Dom pushed back the hair flopping on to his face as he looked up.

'You'll do fine. Lissa, did you say?'

'Yes sir,' she replied with a wicked grin on her face. She managed to refrain from bobbing a small, sarcastic curtsy.

'Sir?' he echoed. 'Forget that. You can call me Dom. I can't do with all this old-fashioned bowing and scraping nonsense. Mind you, I think that's why Elsie walked out, she didn't think it was right for us to be anything more than master and servant. Honestly, did you ever hear such a thing these days? Positively Dickensian. But I suppose it's what my father expected. Now, can you just help me sort out this pile of books? Check I haven't put anything silly into the parcel. Look for the words 'First Edition'. I know my father had quite a number of those.'

Quickly, Lissa looked at the covers. One or two she took out of the pile, to look at in more depth.

'These are going off to one of the London chaps. Middle of the road stuff. Nothing too special here, I believe.'

'This one looks interesting,' she told him. 'Maybe this might be a bit more special?' She had recognised a rather rare edition of a Jane Austen. This man needed some serious help if he wasn't to be cheated out of a lot of money.

'You're right. Well spotted. Heavens. I'm really walking into the wilderness here. Clueless. I can do anything with computers but stick me amongst this lot and I'm hopeless.'

'Perhaps you should get in an expert to make an assessment.'

'They were valued for probate. It seemed like quite a lot of money. But that was a total value and didn't tell me anything about them individually. I suppose I could start trawling the Internet for some dealers. I'd hate for the fruits of my father's favourite recreation to be lost to some cheat, though. But unfortunately, I do need the money.'

'I could look in the phone book. I'm sure there are some reputable dealers in the area.' She knew exactly who should be here looking at this collection but without giving herself away, she could hardly suggest her own father should call at the house. But he did have an agent he used regularly. That shouldn't be too difficult.

'Thanks. Would you mind organising it?'

'Of course. And would you like some tea?'

He nodded absently as she left the

room. If only he could be prised away from the books, Lissa would like to get to know this enigmatic man. He had come of something as a surprise. She hadn't even known the old man had a son. He must have been away at school when they had made their visit.

She phoned the rare books agent and arranged for him to call the next morning. Feeling slightly awkward, she had explained who she was but asked that he should not recognise her when he called.

He obviously found the request a strange one but as she had no intention of being around when he called, she could not foresee any problems. She made some tea and took it into the library.

'I've taken the liberty of asking a Mr Thomas Ashton of Bedford's to call tomorrow morning. About the books?' she told Dom when she put the tea tray down. 'I hope that was OK?'

'You're a marvel. Just what I needed. Someone to take charge of me and organise me. Everyone complains that I'm too absent-minded for my own good. It's just that so many ordinary day to day things don't interest me. Now, tell me all about you. What's a stunning girl like you doing working in some god-forsaken old house like this?'

Lissa grinned. Stunning, was she? That sounded promising.

'Everyone has to work at something,' she replied. 'Earn one's crust and all.'

'You look like you must be very successful.' He eyed her clothes as if he might have recognised the label. Perhaps he wasn't quite as absent-minded as he pretended. 'Fetch another cup and have some tea yourself. Be nice to have someone to talk to. So, how long have you been working for the agency?'

'Honestly? About two-and-a-half hours. Look, I'd better come clean. It's my first job.'

'Aren't you a bit old for a first job?'

'I'm only twenty-three.'

'Precisely. Twenty-three and only just working for the first time? That does sound slightly odd to me.'

'I've been working for my father's business. Unpaid and undervalued. I just wanted a change.'

'And what is his business?'

She paused and looked away. What were the chances of this man knowing her father? He might. The name alone was pretty well-known and hadn't he said he was in computers?

'Oh you know. Imports and exports. Nothing specific.' She wrote off her father's international company with the few words.

He stared at her and she felt herself unexpectedly breathless under such scrutiny. She certainly didn't need to work, not ever, but now she was here, this job meant a lot to her. If only to prove something to her father. Besides, the job certainly had its attractions.

'I think maybe I'd better see about arranging your dinner,' she faltered.

'I insist that you join me. Give us a chance to get to know each. Organise something special and I'll take a wander round Father's wine cellar. See what I can come up with.'

'If you're really sure. Thank you.'

'My pleasure. I hope to find out all about you, Lissa Langham.'

Feeling somewhat shaken, she went to the kitchen. Her heart was pounding in a most uncharacteristic way. Maybe she should have used another name but it was too late now. In for a penny, in for a pound. The only daughter of Alistair Langham had landed a job, entirely on her own merits.

Lissa Settles Into Her Role

Lissa looked for Jane but the girl was nowhere to be seen. She spotted a note on the table and read it quickly. Jane it seemed finished at four. She hoped everything was satisfactory and there was food in the fridge for Mr Wetherill's supper.

Lissa remembered that she actually had none of her possessions with her. Not even so much as a toothbrush. She'd driven over soon after leaving the agency, never giving a thought to the fact she could be starting immediately.

What a pain. She would have to go back home to collect a few things. As for the collection of food in the fridge, two dried up lamb chops was hardly her idea of a gourmet meal. She would call at their own butcher's en route. She knocked at the library door and told Dom of her plans. He looked slightly put out that she had come unprepared but nodded his agreement.

'Don't be too long will you? I'm starving. And I'm rather looking forward to sharing dinner. It's a while since I had company. Shall I open red or chill some white wine?'

'Red. I'll get something suitable to go with it.'

She even felt slightly excited as she drove the ten or so miles to her own home. It was equally as large as Templars, possibly slightly older but in her opinion, very much nicer.

She dashed in through the main door, yelling for Bates as she did so. He was in his sitting room.

'Hello, Bates. It worked. Thank you so much.' She flung her arms round him and he grinned. 'I've landed a job right away and already started. It's a live in, so I have to collect a few things.'

'I'm very pleased m'dear. I hope this doesn't mean I'm to be deprived of my own car for much longer. I really don't like that awkward thing of yours.'

'Oh dear. I don't suppose many housekeepers can afford a Lotus, can they? Whatever shall I do? Of course you must have your car back. I'll just have to get another one. The garage in town will have something, won't they? Just for a few weeks.'

'I'd recommend you might hire something. It would take a long time for everything to be sorted if you buy a new car. Insurance, tax, you know.'

'Oh. I didn't realise. Mine came with everything done for me.'

Bates shook his head. What it was to be young and privileged.

'Can't I just go and collect a new one right away?'

'I doubt it. But hiring one's a definite possibility. I'll make a phone call. See what I can arrange for you. We'll have to hurry though. It's getting late.' He seemed to have entered the spirit of the thing beautifully, thought Lissa. Dear Bates.

'I suppose there's been no message

from Daddy?' He shook his head.

'I'm sorry. No, not a word.' Lissa gave a shrug. They had parted on very bad terms after their row. He had left before she was up the next morning. It was all over nothing at all really, if you didn't count Tony Mason and he had been nothing more than, well a little diversion. A rebellion.

By the time she had cooled off, it was too late and he had left on a trip to the Far East.

She rushed to her room and flung open the wardrobe to pack suitable clothes. All her things were expensive, she supposed. She had rarely taken much notice of cost, usually buying anything that took her fancy. Her father had always been very generous with her allowance.

After her mother died, he had tried to be both parents at once, often spoiling her when he felt guilty about his work taking him away for such long periods. But it had never been about things.

All she had really wanted was his attention. Bates and his wife had largely brought her up, whenever she was at home from boarding school. Occasionally her father had taken her on trips to one of the apartments in Paris or New York but mostly, she had stayed here in their home with Bates and Mrs Bates.

She stuffed a selection of things into a suitcase and grabbed her bag of toiletries. It was near enough to come back for anything she had forgotten and she must surely have time off sometime. She had neither spoken of time off nor money, she realised. And more importantly, she hadn't contacted the agency to let them know she had taken the job. She was quite hopeless, she told herself.

'I've organised a hire car for you,' Bates told her when she went down again. 'I'll drive you to the garage and you'll just need your driving licence and either a credit card or cheque book.'

'You really are a darling, Bates. What would I do without you?'

'Lord alone knows,' he answered. 'I'll

just tell Mrs Bates what's going on.'

'Oh, has she got anything I can cook for supper? I'm too late for the butchers and I'm supposed to make something special. There's only a couple of meagre lamb chops in the fridge there.' She rushed into the kitchen and before Mrs Bates could catch her breath, she had rushed out again with half the contents of the freezer, it seemed.

★　★　★

It took another hour before she was back at Templars. Her hire car was similar to Bates' own car, so she hoped no-one would notice the slight change in colour. She hauled out her suitcase and the bag of food she had taken from home and went to the door.

'Here. Let me help you,' Dom said coming outside to greet her. 'Is that the same car you were in before? I could have sworn it was grey.'

'Er, no. Actually, this is one the garage have lent me. Mine had to have some work done.' Well, it was almost true, she convinced herself.

'And this looks like shopping. We normally have an account with the village shop. You must let me know what I owe you for this lot.'

'I think it was about ten pounds,' she said hopefully.

'You're a strange one,' he murmured. 'Oh Mrs Jenkins phoned. I said you were starting immediately and she was very pleased. Said something about contracts being in the post. Right. What time will dinner be ready?'

'Sevenish?'

'Fine. But you'll have to get a move on. It's already six-thirty.'

'Can we make that eight then?' she asked. He grinned and nodded his head. He looked quite boyish when he smiled. And she hadn't realised how tall he was. She was five feet eight and he seemed to tower over her. It was a nice feeling, looking up to him. His hand brushed hers as he took her suitcase.

'Which room are you using?' he asked.

'Haven't really decided.' He pushed open the first one at the top of the stairs.

'Then I recommend this one. It's large and airy.'

He dumped her suitcase and went downstairs. She took one look around and decided to unpack later. She went down to the kitchen and opened her bag of food to see what there was. She'd managed to pick up one of Mrs Bates' special cheesecakes. That had to impress for the pudding end of the meal.

She set it on a plate and left it to defrost. She'd also managed to pick up some steak and quickly decided on a sauce to go with it, using some of the contents of the fridge.

Once everything was organised, she went in search of the dining room. It was a dark austere room and felt distinctly chilly. She looked in the sideboard for china and cutlery and decided that the warm friendly kitchen was a much better bet.

The scrubbed pine table with a silver candelabra, exquisite cut glass wine goblets, fine bone china and silver cutlery looked slightly incongruous but Dom seemed content enough. He'd changed out of the immaculate jeans he had been wearing into a blue silk shirt and grey trousers. Lissa was glad she'd taken a precious few moments out of her preparation time to freshen her make-up and spray herself lightly with her favourite perfume.

'Mmm, you smell good,' he said as he passed. 'I hope you like claret? This is rather a fine one.' He named one her father enjoyed.

'Oh lovely. A very good choice with the steak.'

'So, you know something about wine too, do you?'

'Only a little. My course, you know. We did some work on what to serve with what.' She must watch that tongue of hers. She was far too quick with her comments about things a housekeeper might not be expected to know about.

'Books, rare or otherwise. Fine wines. And she looks good. Now what more could one want in a companion?'

'Or even a housekeeper?'

He stared at her and she felt herself blushing. She thought again of Tony Mason. How could her father have ever thought she was serious about him? He'd simply been a friend, a small diversion from the excruciating boredom of three weeks at home with no other companionship.

Her father had blown his top, claiming Tony was after her money. It was highly unflattering to be told by her own father that her boyfriends were only taking her out because she was rich. He'd always been the same with any of her friends. Totally over-protective.

The more suitable, rich young men he'd allowed her to meet were so boring that she'd quickly got rid of them. If it was choice of someone rich and dull or poor and interesting, there was no contest. At least Dom Wetherill was seeking her anonymously, with no idea of who she was, or anything of her background. He was also rich, or would be once the estate was settled, so her father certainly could never accuse him of being a gold-digger.

'Now where were you just then?' he teased as her wandering mind returned.

'Just thinking what a lovely change this makes from my usual dull and boring life.'

'A woman with your looks must have boyfriends by the score, all queuing for your attention.'

'Some chance,' she said with a sigh. Not only did she have no real boyfriend in her life, friends of either sex were very thin on the ground. 'I've never really had many good friends of any sort. Erm . . . How are you doing with your book search?' she asked, desperately trying to change the subject. He reached over to refill her glass, just as she was reaching for it. He smiled at her and her heart turned a quick somersault.

'Are you seriously telling me there is no man in your life?'

'Apart from Daddy?' she said before her brain clicked into action.

'I beg your pardon?' Dom said with a piercing glare.

'Sorry, family joke,' she blustered. 'I'm an only child and it's always been the joke that I was Daddy's little girl, after my mother died.'

'Sounds like that was a long time ago.'

'I was only three. I have no memory of her at all. Just a few old pictures.'

'That's tough. You must be very close to your father.'

'At times. He's still having a problem in realising that I've grown up.'

'I suppose all fathers are like that. Especially ones with only daughters. My own father was bad enough with an only son. Never believed I could do anything on my own. Never make my own mark on the world. But, I think I managed to prove him wrong.'

She recognised the situation and gave a wry grin. She tried to prise information from him about his own life but he was reticent to talk about anything more than his current predicament with his father's estate.

'It's a case of finding the best things to retain and preserve for the future and the best way to do it. I'm not really interested in the books, but I feel bad about splitting his precious collection. He saw it as his life's work, in a way. If I put my own money into saving the estate, my company and all the employees could suffer. Catch twenty-two or something. Oh I'm sorry. I must be boring you rigid. Tell me what you like to do. When you're not being a housekeeper,' he added with a wry grin.

The way his hair curled slightly over his collar was quite occupying her concentration.

'I'm sorry. Did you ask what I like to do?' He nodded, smiling again at her lack of concentration. 'I love to ride.

Swim. Reading. Films. All the usual stuff.'

'Tell me what you've seen recently. At the cinema.'

She named one or two movies she had enjoyed and went on to talk about books . . . not the rare variety enjoyed by her father and his, but more the paperback variety. He looked lost. Obviously he neither read nor went to the cinema very often.

'What about computer games?'

'What, firing at aliens and shooting guns? Not my scene at all, I'm afraid.'

'I prefer the more cerebral type of game. The sort where you look for clues and try to work out what the puzzle actually is.'

'Sorry, that's beyond me,' she shook her head. Despite her father's life and work, computers were something one touched only when desperate to send emails, as far as she was concerned.

'Then you must learn. If we are to be friends, you simply must be aware of what I do. That's what my company does. We make computer games.'

Lissa felt her heart sinking. However wonderful this man might turn out to be, she could never put up with another obsessive male. Her father's company had thrived in the computer business and he had been right at the frontline when the boom began. Here she was, dreaming stupid romantic thoughts about another electronics genius.

Lissa and Dom Grow Closer

Thank you. That was a wonderful meal. Loved the cheesecake. Now, we'll find us some brandy and take it through to my study. Then I shall show you the first steps towards your new addiction. I just know you're going to love my latest effort. Come on.' He held out his hand to her and however unwillingly, she simply had to let herself be led away from the kitchen.

'But I really ought to clear up. Dishes and everything. It is my job after all. I'm not being paid to play computer games with my boss.'

He shrugged and waved a careless hand at the mess lying on the table.

'It'll keep. Treat this as your welcome evening. You can't seriously prefer washing up.'

She had to admit he was right. He pushed open the door and led her along the dark corridor to a small room she had barely noticed before. 'Right. You sit there. I'll just boot up.' He moved deftly across her and switched on the computer. She recognised one of her father's most expensive models. She smiled at the coincidence. How long would it be before Dom put two and two together?

He swept out of the room like a rather enthusiastic tornado and came back moments later with a fine decanter and two fine cut crystal brandy balloons.

'If you like movies,' he said, pouring two generous measures in the glasses, 'you are going to be blown away by this.' He pressed several keys and the room filled with music, as a vision of a desert island filled the screen. Waves, incidentally the same colour as his eyes she noticed, broke on a sandy beach. The camera swept round and a building could be seen high on the cliffs. Lissa watched fascinated as an exotic building came into view and a man stepped out of the shadows.

'*My friends, you have returned!*' came the silky tones from the speakers.

'Oh, wow,' exclaimed Lissa. 'That's amazing. Is that really just animation? And that voice . . . is it yours?'

Dom laughed and said it was. He loved taking a role in everything he produced.

'This isn't a major role of course, but like Hitchcock, I always have to be there somewhere. Now. Concentrate. This bit has one of the vital pieces of action. It's wonderful, isn't it?'

'Oh yes,' she breathed. 'Wonderful.' She felt like a teenager on her first date.

Amazingly an hour flew by. She yawned loudly.

'I'm sorry,' she murmured. 'I'm going to have to turn in. I still have to clean the kitchen. What would Jane or the other cleaning lady think if I left that mess?'

'Does it matter?'

'Yes, it does. If I'm to have any sort of credibility, I must at least make a decent impression.'

'You seem very concerned about what people think of you.'

'Look, Dom. I really need to make this job work for me. I've been very lucky to land such a good job on my first application and I want it to go well.'

'OK. But I hope we'll become friends too. What's the point in being highly successful and making pots of money if you never have time to spend it? Like you, I'm rather short on friends. Besides, you aren't supposed to be on duty twenty-four hours a day. Will you allow me to take you out to dinner tomorrow?'

'That would be lovely. But I'm not sure the boss should take his house-keeper out to dinner.' She smiled demurely and he laughed.

'I'll let you get back to your washing up. What time is your book chap coming tomorrow? Oh, by the way, I don't have much for breakfast. Just toast, fruit juice and coffee. Lots of it. Thanks. Have you got everything you need? I'll say good-night then. And thank you.'

'Good night to you too. And thank you too. I really enjoyed this evening.'

Almost an hour later, she crawled into her unfamiliar bed, feeling utterly exhausted but very happy. It felt as if she had suddenly grown up in a way she had never before been allowed. She had got herself a job, of sorts. It may not sound like much of a job to her father but at least she had proved something.

Best of all she had met someone who was very nice. He seemed to like her too, not as some rich girl who might be a stepping stone to a fortune or a career, but for herself. She really needed to boost her confidence. Whatever image she may project to the world, the reality was that she was completely lacking in self-confidence. The view she presented of herself was probably quite insufferable to most people.

No wonder she was so short of friends. She may seem to be a spoiled rich girl but her heart yearned for something gentler, something sincere. She was quite ingenuous if she thought someone like Tony Mason could really like her for herself. Her father was right. He was probably seeing her for her money.

Apart from school, the only people she had really spent time with were her father's friends and various people who worked for them. So much for an expensive education, she thought. It could leave one lacking in far too many ways. But everything was about to change. Twenty-three? It was high time she began to take charge of her own life. Maybe she would make some mistakes. Maybe she needed to make some mistakes.

To her amazement, Lissa awoke before seven and went downstairs. In the kitchen, Dom was already brewing a pot of coffee. It smelt wonderful.

'I'm sorry. I should be doing that.'

'Not a problem. I was awake and thought I could do with a caffeine fix.'

'Me too. I'll put some toast in. Where would you like breakfast to be served?' Lissa asked.

'I'll have it here thanks, I usually do. I've been making my own ever since I came back here, after the funeral. What do you think I should do with this place?' he asked suddenly, changing the subject.

'It depends. On your long term plans.'

'How do you mean?'

'Well, presumably you will marry sometime and want somewhere to live. It could be a wonderful family home.'

'You think so? I always thought it more like a museum than anything. All these fine pictures and works of art. And the books. Speaking of which, I'd like you to help me with the book sorting this morning. Help me to deal with this agent chap. Will you?'

Lissa felt herself blushing. She had planned to be right out of the way when

Mr Ashton made his visit.

That way, there could be no awkward moments.

'I was planning to spend the time working on . . . well, all sorts of things. For instance, I thought I might make an inventory of the household linens. And look at your diary. Do some planning. Probably some shopping. You said a lot of people will be visiting over the new few days. I need to get organised for that. Presumably they will need rooms and food has to be bought and prepared.' She thought that all sounded efficient and the sort of thing a housekeeper might do.

'Very commendable. But I need your expertise this morning. You proved you have certain abilities yesterday and I think that it might be very useful. After all, I would have sent that Jane Austen in a parcel to someone who would never had admitted what he'd got and probably made a fortune from it.'

There was nothing she could do. Helping Mr Ashton may prove tricky but she had to do it. She just had to hope that Thomas would play things her way and not disclose their long acquaintance. When Jane arrived, Lissa told her to do her usual chores and that she would change things in future, if it seemed necessary.

'The post's on the hall table. I usually take it in to Mr Wetherill once he's settled in the library.'

'Fine. As I said. Just carry on as usual. Oh, where's this list of visitors he's expecting?'

Jane handed her a large black diary and she flicked through it to see exactly what she was in for. Fortunately, it seemed that the current week was reasonably clear.

Over the following weeks were various lunch parties and one dinner party. The names of the guests were indicated by initials. A second book was given to her and this provided lists of names to go with the initials. It also recorded when they last attended and what they had been given to eat. Some names were underlined in some sort of colour code. Lissa looked helplessly at Jane.

'What on earth does all this mean?'

'Something to do with who shouldn't sit next to who. And the green lines mean vegetarian, I think. They are friends of old Mr Wetherill. I think Mr Dom is trying to see them all for his father's sake. Lovely man he was.'

'Yes. He was. Well, so I understand,' she blustered. 'Wow. That's some system you have there. Elsie's, I presume?'

'Oh yes. Very organised lady, she was. You'd never dare put a foot wrong with her or you'd be in for the high jump. Not like you. I reckon you and me will get along just fine.'

'Good. Thanks. I hope so. But that doesn't mean I'll accept anything done in a less than satisfactory way.'

'Course not. I'll go and see to upstairs and sort the clean linen, shall I?'

'Right. Yes, of course. Thank you. I'd better get to the library. I'm supposed to be helping sort out the books that are being sold. I might as well take the post as well.' She picked up the bundle of envelopes and took them into the room.

'Your mail delivery.'

'Thanks yes. Leave it on the side, will you?'

She dumped it on to a small table and noticed one of the society magazines was among the delivery.

'Wouldn't have thought this was your scene,' she said glancing at it. He looked up.

'I haven't got round to cancelling all Dad's stuff yet. He would never miss that one. Said it kept him in touch with what's going on in the country. I always thought it was a string of folks wanting their pictures in print.' Lissa said nothing. She was staring in horror at the front cover.

Full Picture Coverage of the Hunt Ball.

She and her father had attended that ball and the wretched photographers had been snapping away all evening. She was probably featured in there somewhere. Perhaps she could hide it away until she had the time to look properly and then, if necessary, she could spirit it away entirely. Gently, she allowed the magazine to fall to the floor, behind the table and turned to Dom.

'Now, what's the plan of action?' she asked brightly. 'Are we just going to let Mr Ashton wander round and pick things at random or do you want to select various items first?'

'What do you recommend?' Dom asked with a slight smile on his face. He had just assumed the man would take out anything he thought valuable and offer a price. He almost blushed at his own naivety.

'Take out one or two of the sets of books. See what he feels about them. Then you can offer some of the rare editions. He'll know what he's looking for. What he can sell. He has clients who want specific items and will be able to match what you have to his own clients. That way, you should be offered a fair price.'

'You're quite something, aren't you? Are you quite sure you're just a housekeeper and not some spy sent in to make a fortune out of my priceless collection?'

She blushed at his words. Surely he couldn't suspect she was a bogus housekeeper? Not so soon?

'I didn't even know where I was going to be sent, did I? How could you suggest such a thing?'

'Hey, I was joking. Calm down or I shall really think there is something odd about you.' His hand was resting on her shoulder and she swung round to look at him. Her green eyes flashed angrily. 'You needn't be so jumpy. I'm not about to sack you.' His eyes were laughing and she relaxed.

'Sorry. OK, I admit it. I'm not exactly a well experienced housekeeper but my talents are so few that I thought it was about all I could do. I do love books

49

though and have made it a bit of a hobby, browsing through old book shops. You can often pick up some bargains.'

It was near enough the truth, she convinced herself. Besides, spending so much time with her father, some things had inevitably rubbed off on her. She enjoyed the thought of all the people who may have leafed through the book before.

'Thanks for your honesty. I really just need someone to take charge of things here and organise the meals for visitors and so on. But I hope you will also be willing to be a friend. Maybe you could help host some of my meals. They are often business clients and old friends of my father too. He specifically asked me to keep in touch with some of them and I feel it's only right.

'I'll try to help wherever I can,' she promised. The doorbell rang and she heard Jane going to answer it. She tapped on the door and opened it.

'Mr Ashton's arrived, sir. Says you're expecting him.'

'Thanks, Jane. Show him in,' Dom said. He stepped forward, his hand outstretched. 'Morning. This is my housekeeper, Lissa Langham.'

'Mr Ashton,' Lissa said politely, shaking his hand. His eyes twinkled with laughter but he said nothing and shook her hand politely. 'I'll go and organise some coffee, shall I?'

'Get Jane to do it. I want you to stay and help. Remarkable lady this one,' Dom told his visitor. 'Knows a great deal about a number of things, including books.'

'Really? Very helpful for you, I'm sure,' smiled Mr Ashton, tactfully.

The trio worked steadily for a couple of hours. Some of the books were simply put on one side with little interest shown but for others, Mr Ashton was most enthusiastic.

'You have some remarkable books in your collection. I suspect that even your father was unaware of the increase in value.'

'I hope the probate valuers were

equally ignorant,' Dom grimaced. 'It would be nice to think I can save at least some of the estate. It's been part of the family for centuries.'

'I have a number of clients who would be most interested in some of the items,' Thomas Ashton said with a sly grin at Lissa. She knew exactly of whom he was thinking.

'Can I offer you some lunch?' Dom asked.

'That's most kind of you. I admit I'd like to spend a lot more time browsing. If it's no trouble, of course.'

'Fine. Lissa will organise something, won't you?'

She stared in surprise. Lunch? Heavens, it was up to her to provide food and drink for everyone. She had quite forgotten, being absorbed in her task.

'Oh yes. Course. I mean, yes. I'll go and sort out some food. Goodness, it's already after midday. The morning's flown by.' She rushed from the room and into the kitchen. Jane and a man and woman were drinking coffee.

'Oh Lissa, this is Mrs Rowley who comes in to help with the cleaning and Harris the gardener. We were just having a break.'

'Fine. Hi all,' she waved a careless hand at the group. 'Sorry, I have to find something for lunch. Dom's invited the book chap to lunch and I hadn't even thought what anyone was going to eat. What does everyone else do about lunch?' Her heart sank as she wondered if she was responsible for feeding everyone.

'Well now, if you're offering Miss, I don't mind if I do have a bite to eat with you. You're a sight better looking than that old misery, Elsie.' The gardener gave a huge grin at Lissa.

'Now then 'arris. Don't you take advantage. We all 'as sandwiches, Miss. Bring them ourselves. Usually eat 'em in 'ere, if that suits.'

'Fine. Now what am I going to feed them on?' She delved in the fridge and brought out some eggs and cheese. There were a few tired lettuce leaves and one tomato. It would have to be a simple omelette and an even simpler salad. Shame there wasn't time to make some fresh bread. 'I'd better go and ask if that's OK for them,' she muttered, rushing out again.

She needed to go shopping. Maybe there was a freezer somewhere? She wasn't used to this sort of thing at all and would much rather have spent the rest of the day with the men in the library, sorting books. There was a steep learning curve ahead, to be sure.

At the end of the day, Dom was happy. After Tom had left, he came to find her and took her hands with a delighted grin.

'You're brilliant. That man was exactly what I needed. He seemed very genuine and suggested prices for some of the books that will help considerably towards securing my future. Now, get yourself dressed up. We're going out to celebrate.'

'But I've got all this to sort out,' wailed Lissa. She had spent an unhappy couple of hours trying to write out menus, with the help of Elsie's old book. 'You've got half a dozen guests coming over next week who already appear to have eaten every delicacy under the sun. In the book it says two of them are vegetarians and don't get on with someone else who might sit next to them. It's all a nightmare.' She felt near to tears.

'I don't have a clue what you're talking about. What book?'

'Elsie's book. She has records of every meal she's cooked and served for the last fifty years, at least.'

'My dear girl. What does it matter who ate what? My guests will be far too polite not to get on with each other. I admit the vegetarian thing is perhaps more important, but you really shouldn't get into any sort of state over it. Come on now. Leave it.'

'Thanks, Dom. You're right. I'll go and change.' She ran up the stairs. What did the silly record books matter? The future looked as if it could be very interesting. Very interesting indeed.

'It Was Just A Simple Kiss'

Lissa flung open her wardrobe doors and stood gazing in despair at the meagre selection of clothes. For a moment she had forgotten she was supposed to be an impoverished house-keeper and longed for some of her more exotic designer labels.

As it was, the best she could manage was a somewhat demure grey silk top and velvet trousers. She had packed them, thinking they would do for any slightly dressier entertaining that might be required. Hardly the thing to wear for a smart dinner somewhere, with a man she desperately wanted to impress. She rummaged in the drawer and produced a bright silk scarf. She remembered the gold chain in her handbag and wound that round her neck. It would have to do.

'I'm sorry,' she apologised. 'I haven't brought much with me. I hope I'm sufficiently smart for you.'

He was wearing a smart dark suit with a blue shirt and tie. He smiled at her.

'You look lovely. But I suppose you'd look good in anything. You're that sort of person. Not one of these model types who always has to be seen in the latest fashion, waving Daddy's cheque book with every step.'

Lissa looked away uncomfortably. He'd hit the target rather too accurately.

'No, it's what's inside that matters. Just what is that perfume you're wearing? I don't recognise it.'

'Oh . . . one of my favourites.'

'It certainly suits you.'

'Thanks. Daddy had it . . . sent it for my last birthday.' She was about to say that her father had had it blended for her specially by someone he knew in Paris. It was her own unique blend and cost a small fortune. Not the sort of thing a temp would wear, she was quite sure. 'Let's go shall we?' She followed him out to his car, a similar model to her own. 'Excuse me, but shouldn't you lock the door?' she reminded him.

'Oh lord. Thanks. I'm so stupid sometimes. You see, I really do need someone practical like you to look after me.'

She gave an ironic smile. Practical? Her?

He leapt up the stone steps and locked the heavy door. 'You'd better take charge of the keys to the main door. I usually use the side door with the spring catch.'

The got into the car and he clicked the seatbelt into place and started the engine.

'Something wrong?' he said anxiously, turning his eyes from the road to look at her.

'Of course not. I was just thinking about my father. We had a row, you see. Before I left. A pretty huge row, actually.'

'Not nice for Daddy's little girl,' he teased.

'Oh please. I should never have mentioned that to you.' She blushed and looked away. She felt his hand reach out for hers and he grasped her fingers, squeezing them gently.

'I'm sorry. Really. I was only teasing. I didn't mean to upset you.' For a moment, she said nothing, not trusting herself to speak. His warm fingers were busily sending pulses of some message to every corner of her body. She almost bit her lip in fear.

'Sorry. I was just having a sensitive moment. All done now,' she said brightly.

'Just as well. Here we are.'

They had stopped outside one of her own favourite restaurants. 'I hope this is OK for you? They do excellent duck here. Some special sauce that's to die for.'

'Great,' was her rather lame response as she slightly panicked inside. She knew several of the staff by name.

Should she confess right away? Or risk some comment from an unsuspecting waiter? 'I think I may have been here before, actually,' she muttered.

'Oh, then you'll know what I'm talking about. I hope you agree with my opinion. It's ages since I went anywhere for a meal. It's no fun dining alone. I think my father brought me here last time. One of the last meals we ever had together. Sorry. I'm getting maudlin. Come on. Let's eat.'

Dom took her arm and steered her gently into the dining room. The waiter was not the usual one. Lissa quietly sighed with relief.

It was a long, relaxed meal. They chatted easily and several times laughed so much that other diners were staring. She didn't know when she'd ever enjoyed herself so much. It was such a relief not to have to look behind her, in case her father might be trying to catch her out. She had never quite realised before, just how suffocating her father's influence seemed to be.

'Thanks, Dom. This has been such a good evening. Lovely food. Excellent company.'

'My pleasure,' he said softly, reaching for her hand. He touched her soft skin, wondering how she managed to keep her hands so soft when she was working. His wonderful eyes looked slightly misty.

'You know, you're not at all the sort of person I would have expected a housekeeper to be. You are intelligent. Well read. Interested in so many things. And you obviously know your way around.'

'Are you implying a housekeeper doesn't need to be intelligent?'

''Course not. Sorry, don't get me wrong. You're just something of a surprise. A very pleasant one, I may add. You certainly weren't my idea of a housekeeper. Especially after the indomitable Elsie.'

As they drove home, Lissa was imagining the next stage in her relationship with this man. There was every opportunity to take things further, if they both wanted it. She gave a small sigh. Her father would have fifty fits if he ever found out exactly what she was doing.

She wondered where he was. If he had called her. She was keeping her mobile phone switched off most of the time in case anyone called at inopportune moments. All the same, she must remember to check it from time to time.

Though she'd hate to admit it to anyone, she had never had any relationship that meant anything, apart from the odd kiss. Daddy was always around if things looked like getting out of hand. In fact, Daddy was always around, full stop.

Despite her sophisticated attitude to most things, she was an innocent in so many ways. Things must not be allowed to get out of her control. She cast another look at the man beside her. He was almost too good to be true. She hadn't yet become accustomed to the strange feeling that stirred deep inside her, every time she merely looked at him.

Some minutes later, she was desperately trying to remember her promise to herself. In the hall, Dom turned to her. He stared at her as if trying to come to some decision. With a tiny sigh, he held his hands out to her, encouraging her to make the next move. She hesitated and moved the tiniest fraction towards him. Immediately, he reached for her and swept her into his strong arms. He held her close and she felt as if she was flying somewhere miles away as gently, he kissed her. He buried his fingers in her hair, sighing as he did.

'I've been longing to do that ever since I first saw you,' he murmured.

Lissa was going through a hundred wildly different emotions. She had never been affected by any man this way before. She wanted his gentle kiss to go on forever.

Then she could hear her father's voice pulling her back. He'd made his speech before she had ever met Tony and she'd tried to ignore the words then. But they kept returning and right now, she thought she could almost hear her father speaking.

Don't allow yourself to be tempted by the first man who flatters you. Anyone you meet will try to tell you you are exactly what he always dreamed of. You're a very beautiful young lady but that apart, you are my daughter. You must learn that men will flatter you to get at your fortune. You're a great catch for someone. I'll always be there to help you and don't you forget it.

'Oh, Dom,' she whispered, moving away slightly. But the ghost of her father's voice was hanging in the air.

'I'm sorry,' he replied a trifle sharply. 'What's wrong?'

'Nothing's wrong. We . . . well, we scarcely know each other.' She dragged her own eyes away from the gaze of his very tempting eyes. She felt herself shiver, hit by the realisation that she felt controlled by her father even at this distance.

'I'm sorry. What's wrong?' he repeated. His eyes misted slightly and he looked at her with genuine confusion. 'I don't understand the problem. The way you responded to me. But I thought . . . I must have been reading the signals incorrectly.'

'I . . . don't get me wrong.' For once she was lost for words. The pounding of her heart was making her feel dizzy and out of control. She was experiencing the most weird feelings of her entire life. 'I really do like you. But it's well, it's too much, too soon.' Her voice tailed away as she felt her cheeks growing pinker and pinker. She looked away. Then she glanced back at him and tried to step back. She cursed her father. Was she ever going to be able to grow up?

'I'm sorry.' His arms dropped and his eyes took on a bewildered expression. The intense blue hardened. 'You gave me every reason to think this was what you wanted.' He paused, annoyed with himself for rushing things. He must have misread the signs. He must be out of practice. He'd been working too hard and what with his father's unexpected death, his emotions must be totally out of control.

He'd blown yet another chance of getting to know someone and this one had to be the most special one he'd ever met. This woman was lighting sparks inside him that he hadn't even known existed. He put a finger under her adorable chin and stared into those remarkable green eyes. There were fresh sparks in the depths. Tiny flecks of gold that he would swear, had only just appeared. She spoke again.

'I'm sorry. It is what I wanted. At least I think so. I'm sorry.' She was babbling, she realised. She must sound like a complete idiot and who would ever want a complete idiot? She couldn't lose this chance of happiness and had to try to repair the damage. 'But I want us to get to know each other. You're a very attractive man. You're everything any woman would want. Good looks. Charm. Money. Obviously, loads of money.'

He could hardly believe what he was hearing. It almost sounded as though she was turning him down because of his money. Not many women did that, not in his experience. He gulped. She surely couldn't be afraid of his wealth? It was usually just the opposite.

'Oh, so that's it. You think because you're my housekeeper, you shouldn't consider yourself good enough? Well that's rot. My position, money or anything else simply don't matter. This is the twenty-first century for heaven's sake.'

He tried to stop himself from sounding a fool . . . but the words came tumbling out. He continued unchecked.

'In my book, people are the important things, not what they're worth on the stock market. You are a beautiful woman and I'd very much like us to get to know each other better.'

How she wished her father could hear this man speaking. How many times had he told her that some man was not a suitable companion, simply because he had no money? Here was Dom, a highly successful businessman, telling her she shouldn't worry about not being financially equal with him. It was almost laughable.

'Thank you, Dom. I'm flattered and delighted. It's nothing like that.' She was too confused even to explain herself properly.

He stepped back, understanding none of her words. She must be making excuses. She had seemed so genuine that he felt deeply hurt, as well as disappointed. He drew in his breath.

'It was just a simple kiss for goodness sake.' He was looking angry. His eyes flashed icy blue chips as he stepped away. He felt rejected, just as he had so many times in life. His mother had left them when he was twelve and he always believed it had somehow been his fault. Boarding school had taught him to become self-sufficient, purely for his own survival.

Any contact with another human being was something he had been forced to learn about the hard way. He'd always been told by his father that he should treat women properly. It wasn't as if his father had been very successful in his own life, relying on inherited money.

As for relationships with women, his father said little. Dom had been determined not to grow up like him, cold and detached, however nice a person he had appeared to all his friends. Dom had discovered that women were attracted to him for different reasons and had very soon learned to discriminate. Gold-diggers were quickly dispatched. As for the rest, they had all been turned away for one reason or another. In the past few years, he had concentrated on developing his business, leaving the personal side of life for later.

'I'm sorry,' she managed to whisper.

He stared at Lissa for several seconds, then took a deep breath and spoke, totally in control again. He brushed his hand through his hair, as if trying to prove that he was keeping everything tidily in its place.

'I'll need an early start tomorrow. See that breakfast is ready by seven-thirty.' He managed to keep his voice calm, hiding the tumult that was affecting him deep inside. He turned and leapt up the stairs, three at a time.

Lissa felt tears burning at the back of her eyes. She wasn't going to cry, in anger or sorrow at the opportunity missed. She had never wanted anyone or anything this much before. She stomped into her own room and shut the door rather more loudly than she should. It was Dom's dismissal of her that finally rankled.

For all his protestations about equality, he had shown that it was somewhat superficial. Who did he think he was? After all, wasn't he planning to sell off his father's book collection to pay the bills? Her own father could probably had written a cheque for his entire expenses without turning a hair. All the time, the ache wasn't going away. She flung her clothes on the floor and took a shower.

Lissa fell heavily asleep around four o'clock. Until then, she had been trying to decide her next move. How could things have got out of her control so quickly? At one moment, she had even toyed with the idea of breaking her cover and admitting exactly who she was, just to set things straight. But she discarded that plan as it would merely prove that her father had been right. She had to stick to this job if only to prove to herself, that she had some small ability. Whatever her current thoughts about her father, she loved him dearly. Her father was a very attractive man himself. For a brief moment she wondered how he had managed on his own all these years.

★ ★ ★

It was almost eight when she awoke to a hammering at her bedroom door. She stretched and called out, 'Go away. I'm asleep.' She rolled over, wondering why on earth Bates should make such a din. Realisation hit her. She flung back the duvet and shot out of bed. She glanced at her bedside clock and remembered that Dom had asked for breakfast by seven-thirty. Some housekeeper she was.

'I'm sorry,' she called, 'I'll be there in a minute.' She flung her clothes on and splashed cold water on her face. She dragged a brush through her hair and knotted it back with a clip and rushed downstairs.

'I'm so sorry . . . I . . . ' She stopped in her tracks as she saw the kitchen table. Breakfast was set out for two, with a small vase of fresh flowers in the centre of the table. The air was fragrant with fresh coffee and Dom was standing, holding on to a chair ready for her.

'I'm sorry, Lissa. I was rude to you

last night. And possibly, I admit I was guilty of trying to rush things. I suppose I wanted to make the most of the moment, before it disappeared again. I don't usually behave that way, I assure you. I've made a mess of too many relationships in the past . . . putting things off for work or something else I considered important at the time.'

'I . . . I'm sorry I didn't get your breakfast ready,' she murmured feebly. 'I didn't sleep very well and then I must have dozed off rather too heavily. This all looks wonderful. Thank you.'

'Do I take it I am forgiven for being rude?'

' 'Course. And I promise I'll try to be a better housekeeper in future.'

After breakfast, Dom disappeared into the library to delve amongst his books once more. Lissa took out Elsie's notebooks once more and tried to come to terms with the complex thinking of the former housekeeper. She was still sitting among dirty breakfast things when Jane arrived.

'Morning,' she said brightly. 'Not still trying to fathom Elsie's system, are you?'

'Afraid so. I think I shall have to abandon it, though. Apart from sorting out the vegetarians, I shall just follow my instincts as far as seating and feeding this lot are concerned.'

'Did you want me to clear the breakfast things?' Jane asked, looking with some interest at the collection of dishes. 'You have your breakfast with Mr Wetherill then, do you?'

'I was a bit late this morning so we sat down together.' Lissa didn't miss the rather curious stare.

Evidently, she was not behaving quite as a housekeeper should. She didn't imagine Elsie had ever shared any sort of meal with her boss. What Jane would have thought about her going out with Dom for the evening, she dreaded to think. Or Lettie Jenkins come to that. She would certainly have disapproved of such familiarity.

'Right, I'll get on then.' Jane began to

clear the table and noisily stacked the dishes into the dishwasher. Lissa put away the books and found a notebook of her own. She would conduct a stock take of the freezer, which she had finally discovered in the utility room. She needed to see exactly what was in there and begin to make her lists for the lunch parties the following week.

At least she felt on comfortable territory there. She could produce as good a meal as anyone and was determined to use the occasions to prove her worth.

When she went into her room some time later, she was shocked to find that her clothes were still scattered around the floor and the wet towels still lay in the bathroom, where she had dropped them. Blast, she muttered, realising that it was now up to her to tidy up after herself and possibly Dom, the way Bates and Mrs Bates had always looked after her. She grimaced and got to work.

She assumed that there was a washer

somewhere and she should probably collect up all the dirty washing. Or was that Jane's duty? She didn't want any mistakes. She took her own used towels downstairs, deciding to ask Jane to specify their different roles. She made some coffee for the two of them and asked her to sit down.

'Jane, you must realise I'm rather new to all of this. I'd like you to tell me exactly who does what in the household. For instance, who does the washing?'

'Well, either me or Elsie did it. Depending on what else was happening. Old Mr Wetherill needed quite a bit of looking after, especially towards the end. There wasn't so much entertaining done then, so Elsie did launder most of his things for him. I don't really mind what I do. Mrs Rowley does most of the cleaning of course and Harris the gardening. He cleans the cars as well and looks after the rubbish.'

'I see. So it's sort of up to us to agree what we do?'

'I 'spect so. Since Mr Dominic's been here, everything's got a bit disorganised. He seems to think he can come into the kitchen whenever the mood takes him. Even makes his own coffee sometimes. That's partly what Elsie couldn't cope with. She expected him to be the same sort of gentleman his father was. Lovely man. Real gentleman.'

'As distinct from me?' Dom's voice came from the doorway.

'Oh sir, I'm sorry. I didn't mean anything by it. I'm sure you're a gentleman too.' Poor Jane was covered in blushes and confusion.

'It's OK. No offence taken. But I should appreciate some of that coffee. And I could do with your help in the library, Lissa. If you have the time, of course.'

'I'll bring you some coffee into the library.'

Dom left the room and Lissa grinned at Jane. 'Don't worry about it. Dom won't take offence. Would you mind taking the washing out of the machine when it's done? I suspect I'm about to become his book advisor once more.' Jane smiled and nodded, glad to escape from her embarrassment.

Lissa and Dom spent the rest of the day sorting through the never-ending shelves of books. They had sandwiches at lunchtime, as they continued to work. Realising she had extensive knowledge, Dom asked her advice before placing any books in any of the various piles. It was companionable and productive, working this way. More than once, they touched hands as they were taking books from each other. She could see that her boss was trying very hard not to upset her in any way and she smiled at his thoughtfulness. Still, he was something of a dream catch for any woman. His handsome face had an appeal that was not difficult to define.

'Hey! I was asking about this group. Where on earth were you just then?'

'Maybe nowhere on this earth,' she

replied with an enigmatic smile on her lips.

'Well don't look like that too often or I may find it impossible to keep my resolution.'

'And what resolution is that?'

'The one you wanted to impose on me. Not to rush you. Us. Take things easy.'

She bit her lip, preventing herself from urging him not to take things too easy. She was a mass of conflicting emotions. Perhaps it was the unaccustomed freedom from her father's supervision. All the same, she might have been glad of her father's advice on this occasion.

'Sorry. Yes. Which group of books were you talking about?'

He smiled gently, as if sensing her inner thoughts.

They returned to their work and the moment was over. She forced herself to concentrate. Jane came in with tea at some point of the afternoon, announcing that she was about to leave.

'Thanks a lot, Jane,' Lissa said absentmindedly. 'See you tomorrow.'

'It's Saturday tomorrow. Nobody comes in of a Saturday, unless there are visitors, of course. I might be able to arrange it though, if you need me.'

'Oh no. That's not necessary. I'm sure we can manage, can't we?'

Dom nodded.

'Right, well if there's nothing else,' Jane said. 'I'll leave you to it.' She shut the door firmly behind her.

'There's Never Been Anyone Special'

Shall we eat out or at home tonight?' Dom asked Lissa at six o'clock when they'd eventually finished with the books.

'You don't have to feel you need to share every meal with me. I can always cook something just for you.'

'I told you, I dislike eating alone.'

'I'll cook something then. Besides, if you're so broke you need to sell your father's books, you need to economise. Less meals out for a start.'

'Don't nag. Besides, I'm not exactly broke. I just want to find the best way to pay the taxes. I'm really trying hard to keep my company out of the equation. I don't want to mix the two. But, if it turns out that I need to, I can spend some capital on this place. We can still go somewhere nice to eat, if you'd like to.'

'Actually, I quite fancy another look at that game of yours. I haven't seen anything like that before. How do you fancy pasta with my special pepper sauce?'

'Sounds wonderful. I'll find a bottle of something to go with it.'

'Something Italian would be good. Won't take too long.' She went into the kitchen and began to search for her ingredients. She'd seen plenty of dry stores in the pantry and knew there were various items in the freezer that would add the extra flavours. She also needed some red wine, not one of the vintage bottles from the cellar but something to add a zing. She foraged round and found a wine box in the pantry.

She laid the table in the kitchen once more, reminding herself to ask Dom where he really preferred to eat. She hummed gently as she worked, enjoying the prospect of another evening in the company of this man who was beginning to mean so much. The red sauce bubbled in the pan as she was struck by a thought.

Could it be that she was beginning to fall in love with him? She'd never before been close enough to anyone to consider love. She'd never been allowed to be close enough to anyone, thanks to her father. Naturally, she loved her father and believed he loved her, but that was entirely different.

As a child she'd quickly learned exactly how to manipulate her father to buy her things she thought she wanted. It was partly blackmail to make up for the fact that he was always too busy to give her as much time as she should have had. Somehow, she didn't think she would be able to make Dom do anything he didn't want to do.

She felt excited just at the thought of Dom. If all these feelings were indeed love, then she must be falling in love. It was a wonderful feeling and she was determined to make the most of it.

'How's it going?' Dom asked as he came into the kitchen. 'Smells sensational. This do?' he asked, holding out a bottle of Chianti. 'No disputing it's Italian . . . maybe a trifle obvious but it was the first one I found.'

'That's fine. Good year. Just at its best, I'd say.' She spoke rather too fast, as if it was necessary to hide her earlier thoughts.

'You do know a remarkable amount about all sorts of things. Whatever you try to pretend, I believe there's more to you than being an agency temp. Why won't you tell me more about your background?' This was dangerous territory.

'I'm fairly boring. Did OK at school. Never fancied university. Dad was always travelling and I tagged along sometimes. I picked up a bit of knowledge en-route, of course. Then I took my cookery course and now I'm using what I learned. That's about it really. Now, are you ready for this food? I hope it's OK to serve it in the kitchen?

Or would you prefer the dining room?'

'I told you before. I'm much happier in here.'

Despite spending most of the last two days together, there still seemed plenty to talk about. Lissa's only problem was not to say anything that gave too much away about her own background. She had to be certain that the undoubted attraction they both felt, was genuine and nothing to do with her own fortune. If this was going to work out the way she hoped, she could prove to her father that it was her, not his money that was the attraction.

'I'll help you clear up,' Dom offered unexpectedly. 'Then you won't complain that I'm keeping you from your duties. I've loaded the game on to the computer so we can go and play right after we finish here.'

They were remarkably efficient in their work and soon the kitchen was looking immaculate.

'Pity Jane won't be here tomorrow to see how neat and tidy we've made the place,' Dom said with a wry grin. 'I doubt even Elsie could fault the state of her precious territory. Now, let's see how the world of Narl is getting on, shall we?'

It was several hours later before they decided to call it a night.

'Gosh. I never thought I'd become a computer junkie. This is such a wonderful game. You are very talented, Dom. This one has to be a best seller.'

'I certainly hope so. Though I can see one or two defects already. You have shown me some of the snags and I'm grateful. I needed someone who wasn't too used to playing the games, just so that I could see exactly how it worked out. I shall have to put you on to the company payroll.'

He had spent the entire evening watching her. He adored the slight wrinkle of her nose as she concentrated on his game. He wanted to touch her hair, stroke the back of her neck. He didn't want to spoil things in any way however difficult that may be. He knew he must be patient and wait for her to give the next cue.

'I think my lack of sleep last night must be catching up on me. I'm very tired,' Lissa said, at last. 'Thanks for a lovely evening. And a good day too. I really enjoyed myself.' Each day they spent together, a little more they knew about each other.

They went upstairs and politely said their goodnights. She went into her room. She shut the door and leaned against it. She heard Dom's door shut and relaxed. She went to shower and get ready for bed. Lissa climbed into bed and pulled the duvet over her and did her best to fall asleep. It wasn't easy.

★   ★   ★

The weekend passed peacefully and companionably. Dom insisted she took some time off on Sunday and she drove back to her home. Bates and Mrs Bates were sitting out in the garden. When her car stopped outside, they leapt to their feet anxiously, as if afraid they were being caught out.

'Please, stay where you are,' Lissa called. She pulled up a chair and sat beside them.

'Can I get anything for you?' Mrs Bates asked anxiously. 'Tea or something?'

'In a while. Let's just sit here and chat for now. How are things? Any news of my father?'

'Not a word. I expect he's busy somewhere. I did speak to someone from the London office and she said he was planning to go to the Far East soon. He may be in Paris. Would you like me to try the number and see if he's there?' Bates offered. 'He usually stays at the apartment.'

'No, don't bother. I expect he'll be in touch when he's ready. I do keep checking my mobile. Just in case.'

'You mustn't let it upset you, love,' Mrs Bates said kindly. 'I think maybe the pair of you are a bit too much alike, you know. That's why you sometimes have a bit of a falling out.'

'I know. He simply doesn't realise I've grown up. I am capable of making my own decisions. I'm even holding down a job, aren't I?'

For the next few minutes, she talked about her role as housekeeper, as if it were something completely new. Mrs Bates hid her own smiles, as the girl she'd known all her life was finding all about her own job, for the first time. Maybe it would be the making of her, to discover all the things she took for granted. Much as she loved Lissa, the girl did take a lot of things for granted.

'And what about the owner of the house? Is he nice? Good to work for?' She watched the reaction as Lissa enthused for several minutes. 'So, you like him a lot, do you?'

'Well, yes, I suppose I do.'

'Just be careful, love. You never know with these odd business types. He may take you for granted.'

'Dom Wetherill? No, he'd never do that. Far from it. Not the old-fashioned type like his father. Not one little bit. We always eat together and in the kitchen, unless he's entertaining.'

'Is he anything to do with old Mr Wetherill? Your father's friend from Templars?'

'Dom's his son. Thought you knew that. Not that I should be telling you this, I suppose. Oh, but he's such a nice man. No pretensions. And looks to die for. His hair's so black and his eyes are quite a remarkable colour. Sort of azure blue.'

'I see,' smiled the old lady. 'Well, at least he's from a decent background this time.'

'What do you mean? This time?' Mrs Bates gave a knowing smile. It appeared she knew a lot more than Lissa had realised. 'I think that tea might be nice, now.' Obviously, it was necessary to change the subject. 'I want to collect a few more clothes to take over. I won't be long. Then I should get back. I have

90

to think of something to cook for supper.'

'I've got a couple of nice salmon steaks, if you'd like them. Save you a bit of time. And there are some fresh peas in the garden. We could pod them while we have our tea.'

'Thanks so much Mrs B. I don't know how I'd ever manage without you. But I am managing, aren't I? Quite surprisingly well, actually. Oh, I did mean to ask. Does it matter what temperature you wash silk in? I stuck my shirt in with the sheets and it's gone a bit strange looking. What should I do with it?'

Mrs Bates smiled happily. Her little girl wasn't quite as grown up as she thought she was.

'You'd best bring it back here and I'll see if there's something I can do with it. No promises but I'll have a go.'

Managing on her own, was she? The old lady gave her a fond smile and sighed happily. She couldn't quite manage without her old Mrs Bates.

'Can you bear another session on the computer tonight?' Dom asked anxiously when she arrived back.

'If you like. Why do you sound so anxious?'

'I want to sort out one more section of the game and I need you to see if it works the way I propose.'

'OK by me.'

'You're a star,' he said grasping her arm and squeezing it gently. 'Sure you don't mind?'

His touch had set the nerves tingling again. His hand lingered and she found herself actually staring in fascination at the movement of his long fingers.

'Sorry,' he murmured, letting go.

They were in the midst of the game some hours later when an ominous bang came from the back of the computer. The whole thing shut down and made several fairly terminal sounding clicks and hisses.

'Oh, I don't believe it.' Dom slapped

his hand on the desk in frustration. 'How'm I supposed to work when something like this happens? I doubt they'll manage to get anyone out to me for ages.'

'Can't you look at it? You're into computers. Surely you can do something?'

'I'm no more than a glorified programmer. I write codes, basically. I don't know enough about the workings to start messing about inside. Besides, I have a contract with the manufacturers. They'll have to be called out to fix it. I can't be without my machine. I've too much to do.' He was pacing around as if he'd been mortally wounded.

'I'm sure someone will get to you as soon as possible,' she tried to reassure him.

'You know nothing about these companies. Once they've supplied the goods, they don't care about anything any more.'

'Surely not. I've heard they do a lot of after-sales cover.' She stopped, realising she was angrily trying to defend her father's company. She'd heard it all for years, the comments about people who bought computers and broke them through sheer ignorance.

It was a major problem to try and sort them all out, especially when they seemed to expect the whole thing should be done for no extra cost to the customer. All the same, she was certain that in this case, it was some fault with the machine itself rather than something that had been done incorrectly.

'Haven't you got a laptop? You could work on that.'

'I use it for other stuff. I can't afford to start messing about with games on that. I wouldn't risk being out of touch with everything else. I bought this machine thinking it would do its job.'

'I'm sure it will, when properly maintained,' she said huffily. She felt loyalty demanded she stood up for her father's products. He gave her a curious stare.

'I thought you knew nothing about computers.'

'I don't. But they always say a bad workman blames his tools. I was only remembering that.'

He frowned slightly but gave a shrug rather than say any more. She certainly was a strange one.

'I'll get on the phone first thing. But, I'm afraid that's it for tonight. We'll both have to curb our impatience for the conclusion of the game. This is serious stuff to me. It's my life.'

She stared at him, wondering if he was trying to say something in an oblique way.

'I expect there's a long line of your conquests lurking around.'

'My conquests?' He gave a wry grin. 'No. There's never been anyone special. Truly.'

'Yes, well you have the advantage over me. Anyone at all would be something. Special or not.'

'Really? I find that hard to believe. A gorgeous girl like you.'

'Yes, really. Just the occasional drink out with someone but nothing serious, ever. My . . . ' She stopped herself from admitting that it was her father who put a stop to just about everything and everyone who ever came close to her. She felt herself blushing furiously.

'Hey, it doesn't matter. Please don't look like that.' He placed a finger under her chin and lifted her face towards his. 'As I say, I'd never push you into anything. Not unless you want to. Now, let's say goodnight. I'll see you in the morning.'

'Night,' she called as she fled up the wide staircase.

Could he be the one man she'd been waiting for all her life? Her emotions were jangling and she wasn't being rational any more. Her father wasn't here to put her off any feeling she might have for anyone. With pursed lips, she switched on her mobile to see if her father had left a message. There was nothing.

It was up to him, she thought. She

96

was not going to make the first move. He owed her an apology, she firmly believed. Maybe her father was finally losing his hold over her. Was she fighting something she needn't fight any more?

* * *

She was up early the next day and for once, breakfast was ready when Dom came into the kitchen. The tension she had been feeling the previous evening seemed to be over. He was anxious about his precious computer and seemed to be fully occupied by thoughts of getting someone here to look at it. He ate quickly and was soon telephoning the service department of her father's company.

She realised that whoever came to sort it out might easily be someone she knew. It was most probably someone she'd know. She'd spent a lot of time in her father's office during her life and knew most of the regular people. She'd just have to make herself scarce and let Jane answer the door. With any luck, she needn't even see the engineer. She set to work to prepare for the first of the luncheon parties in two days' time.

There was another the following day and a dinner at a date to be confirmed. The second two were smaller affairs, each for Dom and two guests. She had planned the menus and ordered the ingredients to be delivered the next day. There was plenty to do, including sorting the china, cutlery and glass. Most of it hadn't been used for months and so it all needed a good wash. The dishwasher could cope with the china but the silver and glass needed careful handling and polishing.

More than once, she wished Bates was here to help. He was marvellous with silver and for a rash moment, wondered whether to load it into her car and drive it over for a dose of his expert treatment. But that would hardly be coping with her job on her own. In the midst of her thoughts, the doorbell jangled. She waited, expecting Jane to answer it. But it rang again. Cursing, she went into the hall. She opened the door.

'Hello . . . Lissa! What a surprise. What are you doing here?' Alan, one of the engineers she knew very well, was standing on the doorstep.

'Ssh,' she hissed. 'You don't know me. All right?'

'If you say so. I'm here for Mr . . . Mr Wetherill. Computer problems, I gather.'

'You'd better come in. Mr Wetherill's in the study, nursing his sick computer. I'll show you the way.' She turned and saw Dom watching them. Had he overheard anything, she wondered? 'Oh there he is. I'll leave you to get on with it. Shall I bring some coffee?'

'Thanks. That would be great.'

Hoping her cover hadn't been blown, she carried a tray of coffee into the study. She wondered where Jane had disappeared to, wishing she could have sent the girl in with the coffee. She set the tray down and poured two cups.

Automatically, she spooned two spoons of sugar into Alan's cup, remembering how he liked it from the numerous cups she had made for him in the past. He was one of the most senior of the engineers. Obviously he had been sent to this job as such a good client deserved the best.

'Do you actually like two spoons of sugar?' Dom asked curiously, watching as Lissa had poured the coffee and added sugar.

'Exactly right. Thanks, Lissa.'

'You're welcome,' she answered with a glare. Alan gave a start. He'd probably let some sort of cat out whichever bag she was playing with.

'Do you two know each other from somewhere?' asked Dom.

'Course not. He must have heard you using my name. There's your coffee, Dom. Black and no sugar. See? I know these things. Part of my job. Most engineers take two spoons of sugar. It's a statistic. I read it somewhere. Now, you must excuse me. I have lots to do.'

She simply wasn't clever enough to play her role. She was not used to pretending about anything.

She was aware of Dom's eyes following her out of the room but was reassured as she heard Alan talking easily about some technical point with the computer.

Dom Does Some Investigating

The computer problem was fixed with minimal trouble. 'Good chap, that one,' Dom told her. 'Are you really certain you didn't know that engineer? Socially? Any other way? You seemed to have some sort of rapport.' He was aware of a ridiculous feeling of jealousy that anyone else might know this woman.

She shook her head. He continued to stare at her and then gave a shrug of acceptance. 'I must say, I was afraid it was something much more serious when I heard that bang last night. But, thanks to Alan's talents, we're in business again.'

'That's great. I assume I shall be able to see what happens next to the mighty Narl, this evening.'

'If you like. I wondered if we might

102

eat out and have the chance for a talk.'

'Nonsense. There's nothing we can say in a restaurant that we can't say here.'

'Whatever you fancy.'

But she could see that Dom was still troubled by something. He went into the study and she heard the click of the phone. She tried to listen to what was being said, but the door was too thick. She tried questioning him later, surreptitiously asking about his day, trying to discover whom he'd been calling but he would let nothing slip.

She was being paranoid, she told herself. All the same, some sixth sense told her that the call had been something to do with her.

★   ★   ★

During the afternoon, it began to rain. The warm weather they had been enjoying for a while had suddenly broken. It was a July storm with a vengeance. As evening fell it became dark ridiculously early. Dom emerged from his study and found Lissa in the kitchen.

'What weather,' he complained. 'I thought I'd better unplug the computer and modem, in case it thunders.'

'It's certainly hot enough for thunder. I was just trying to decide what to cook this evening.'

'So, you're sure you don't want to go out?'

'I think we should probably stay in. Even between car and restaurant we could get soaked.'

As it turned out, it was a good decision. When the first clap of thunder came, the rain came down even faster. They could hear water cascading down over the gutters and clattering down on the slate terrace.

'Blasted gardener,' Dom moaned. 'I keep telling him to clear the gutters but he's always got something more important to do. I often wonder what he actually does do. Maybe you can tell him next time he's here.' Lissa was standing by the window.

'Where does the water drain to? Off the terrace, I mean.'

'Not sure. On to the lawn, I suppose. There are drainage holes at the bottom of the wall.'

Lissa frowned as she was peering out of the window.

'I don't want to worry you, but I think there could be a problem.' The next flash of lightning illuminated what looked like a lake outside. The terrace was filling rapidly and the water seemed to be lapping at the French windows of the lounge. Dom stood behind her and peered out into the darkness. The lightning dutifully flashed on cue and lit up the growing scene of devastation. The rain was hammering down and even the tubs of flowers were beginning to look like small water features.

'Who needs a water feature when you can have the whole of Buckinghamshire in a British summer?' Dom said grumpily.

'Do you think we should do something? Put sandbags down or whatever it is one does.'

'Have you got any sandbags?' Dom's voice was scornful. 'Sorry. You're right. I suppose the first thing is to discover why the water isn't flowing away. I'll find some wellies and go and have a poke around.'

He went into the utility room and selected a pair of boots from the rack. He pulled on a long jacket and sou'wester and opened the door. The wind practically pulled it off its hinges and the rain blew in like a hosepipe pressure spray.

Lissa went into the lounge to see if there was any water damage. A small trickle under the French window was beginning to grow larger. It had already reached the edge of the carpet, a rather good Persian square which covered much of the floor.

Quickly, she pushed the furniture away and rolled it back. Towels, she muttered to herself and rushed upstairs to the linen cupboard. She grabbed all she could carry and took them down to lay across the bottom of the window. At least that might stop the water from spreading too quickly. It wouldn't do much good to the polished wooden floor beneath but doubtless someone would know what to do to restore it. The main task now was to get the water flowing away from the house.

As she went into the utility room, Dom was returning. The door flew open and what seemed like jets of water sprayed into the room. She ducked back away from the blast of water.

'I need something to poke through the drain holes. They all seem to be blocked.' Lissa glanced round. She saw a mop and broom and grabbed them.

'You can use the handles. I'll be with you in a sec.' He went outside again and she turned to the boot rack. She saw several pairs of smaller boots and found some that would almost fit. She also found some waterproofs, several sizes too large.

She followed Dom into the worst of the storm. Round the side of the house, it was like walking into a waterfall. The gutters were overflowing and the sheer volume of rain was causing the ground to flood. There was simply nowhere for the water to go. Lissa felt herself panicking slightly. She didn't know whether to go back inside and try to find something to stem the flow of water going into the house or go to help Dom. Despite her fears, she decided on the latter. She fought her way to the terrace and clutching her mop, tried to ask him to direct her to the gaps in the wall.

Their voices were lost in the howling winds and lashing rain. He signalled to her to try and push water down the steps. He handed her the broom and she began to make what seemed like futile gestures to push the water away. Her arms felt like lead as she kept pushing, pushing against what seemed like a rising tide. Dom had managed to clear some places and almost imperceptibly, the water began to drain away.

Lissa was soaked through. The large mac she had found was flapping around so much in the wind, it was almost worse wearing it than getting wet without it. In frustration, she finally flung it on to a half submerged seat. At least the weather was still reasonably warm, though in seconds, the teeming rain soaked right through her tee-shirt and jeans.

Feeling totally exhausted with what seemed a futile battle, she was near to tears. Housekeepers shouldn't have to cope with this, she grumbled to herself but continued to sweep. The rain was falling as heavily as ever. Dom came to join her efforts. His powerful arms seemed to make a much greater impact and the water gradually began to go down. She gave him a feeble smile of gratitude.

'You go in,' he yelled above the din. 'See if there's any damage inside.'

'I'd rather stay here and help you,' she yelled back. 'I've put towels down in the lounge.'

'Sorry? I didn't catch that.'

'Never mind.' It was hopeless. She continued to sweep at the torrents of water. The thunder was slowing down and the lightning disappearing into the distance. It seemed like several hours later, the rain began to subside. Stumbling with weariness, Lissa staggered back to the utility room. She began to shiver as soon as she had stopped her physical efforts.

She tried to heave off the sodden boots but they seemed stuck firmly, with the wet inside as well as outside. She sat on the floor and tried again. Her tears were flowing unchecked by now. It was a combination of exhaustion and frustration. Dom came in and found her slumped against the wall.

'Lissa. Lissa, whatever's the matter?'

'I'm sorry. I can't get my boots off,' she sobbed. 'And I'm soaked to the skin. And it's still raining. And the lounge floor and carpets are probably ruined.'

'You poor love. Come on. Stick up

your foot. I'll try to pull the boots off.'
He grasped one foot and tugged hard.
With a loud sucking noise, her foot slid
out and water poured out of the leaky
boot all over her legs and then on to the
floor. 'Sorry,' Dom said as he stifled a
smile. 'Give me the other.' The same
thing happened and Lissa also managed
a rueful smile. 'Now you can do the
same for me,' he invited.

She hauled herself to her feet and
pulled at Dom's boots. There was less
of a problem as his were at least one
size too large.

'Why didn't you find a mac or
something?' Dom asked as he peeled
off. his own sodden outer garments.

'I did but it was flapping too much. I
left it outside.'

'Well, I'm not volunteering to fetch
it. But you're soaked. You should go
and take a hot bath and have some
brandy to get you warm from the
inside. Come on.'

'But I'm dripping everywhere. At
least there's a stone floor in here. It will

ruin the parquet floors in the rest of the house.'

Just when they thought things were returning to normal, the power went off.

'I'll put the kettle on and make some coffee,' Dom said as he groped his way into the kitchen.

'Oh yes. And what will you use for power?'

'Ah,' he replied. 'Silly how one doesn't think. Pity we don't have gas.'

'I won't be able to have a shower either. They're all electric, aren't they?'

'You can have a bath, though. The water should still be hot. You can light candles and sip some brandy. Treat yourself to a taste of luxury.'

In the darkness, Lissa felt her wet body growing goose bumps. She shivered and called to Dom.

'I'll see you in a while. I won't use all the hot water. I expect you'll need a bath too.' She ran up the stairs as fast as she dared in the darkness.

There was the remains of a candle in

one of the drawers in her room. It had been left by some previous occupant, together with a match book. She groped to find it and struck a match. She lit the candle and stood it on the side of the bath as she ran the steaming water.

The heat soon penetrated her cold skin and she felt the blood beginning to course round her body once more. She realised there was silence outside. The rain had finally stopped. Once the power came on, they would need to examine the floors inside the house to see if there was any damage.

Then, she supposed, she needed to think about food. Not that she was hungry, but after all their efforts, they needed to replenish their energy. There could still be a great deal of work ahead.

By the time she had finished her bath, the power was restored. She went to the kitchen and began to prepare something for them to eat. She put soup to heat and made sandwiches.

When Dom appeared, his hair curling damply around his sweatshirt, she even managed a wan smile.

'Just getting something to eat. Shall we inspect the damage first or eat first?'

'I'd better go and take stock first,' he decided.

She followed him round the house. The lounge carpet was only slightly damp at one edge. Her efforts with the towels had been reasonably successful. He tried to pick one of them up but the water dripped out.

'We need something to put them in. Have we got a large tub or something?' Dom asked.

She went to look in the utility room but there was nothing suitable. She grabbed some dustbin sacks and took them. They soon stuffed all the towels in and examined the floor beneath. Several of the parquet blocks had risen and were lying at odd angles. Dom gazed at it in horror.

'I reckon this whole floor will probably have to be taken up. This amount of water can soak in every-where. We'd better look in the other rooms. The library should be OK. At least that's on the other side of the house. But we may need to get some dehumidifiers going. Make sure the damp doesn't damage anything. I'd better see if I can get some delivered first thing in the morning.'

'Aren't you insured? Surely you must be.'

'Of course. But I expect there will be loss adjusters and no end of hassle. We shall have to cancel the lunch parties. Well, postpone them at least.'

★   ★   ★

The next morning, they were both up early. The full extent of the devastation could be seen. The entire garden was covered in debris. The water had subsided, leaving a track of mud and sludge across the usually immaculate lawns. The once colourful flower tubs were totally wrecked and stones and more mud littered the terrace.

The borders at the bottom of the lawn were a mass of fallen bushes, dragged out by the flood of water and the tearing winds. Inside the house, there was no more apparent damage than they had seen the previous night. The utility room looked the worst. It was full of wet towels, mud and the soaking garments they had worn. By the time they had eaten the previous night, they had both been too exhausted to cope with any of it.

'Mrs Rowley will help out and Jane will be here soon,' Dom comforted.

'But don't we have to leave everything until the insurance people have been?'

'You're right. I'll phone right away. What would I do without you?'

'Dom, it's only seven o'clock. Nobody will be in their offices for hours yet. Come on. Let's organise some breakfast.'

Companionably, they sat together drinking coffee and eating toast. Lissa was struck by the thought that they seemed like an old married couple. She stifled a grin, thinking how inappropriate were her thoughts.

All the same, she was proud of herself for the way she had coped. Once, she would have simply expected someone else to repair the damage and she would probably have cursed because her plans for the evening had been spoilt.

When Jane arrived, she was shocked and almost burst into tears herself.

'All the lovely garden. Mr Harris will go ballistic. It's ruined. And the poor house. Still, I suppose it could have been much worse. You poor things, having to cope with all that. And there's the parties going off this week. Whatever shall we do?'

'Postpone them of course. We can't even start to clear up until the insurance people have been,' Lissa told her. 'Put some of the towels in the washing machine and then maybe you should make a start upstairs, until we know what's happening.'

Dom spent his time phoning various people and didn't appear for much of the morning. To her consternation, Lissa discovered later exactly whom Dom had phoned the previous day. It seemed like years ago, she thought. She answered the phone herself when Dom let it ring, expecting to hear the insurers.

'Is that Miss Langham?' said the vaguely familiar voice.

'Speaking.'

'Lettie Jenkins here. I had a call from Mr Wetherill yesterday. I must say, it did give me some concern.'

'Oh. Good morning Mrs Jenkins. Whatever did he say? I thought Mr Wetherill was quite satisfied with my work.'

'Oh, I believe he is. But I must say, I do have some slight worries about your references. I'd like you to call in at the office today, at your convenience.'

'But I'm extremely busy today. We were flooded last night. I can't possibly leave the house at all. There's so much mess everywhere. We're waiting for the insurance company to come to make an estimate.'

'Very well, but I must insist on seeing you in person. We'll leave it until next week then. Thursday afternoon would suit me best. I do understand your current problem. Oh, you needn't be concerned that you are being dismissed. But you have to understand, I have my reputation to think of. The meeting is merely a formality, so you needn't worry unduly.'

But despite the reassurance, Lissa did worry. What on earth could Dom have said to the woman? She decided she must broach the subject with Dom himself.

'Whatever did you say to her?' she demanded after telling him of the phone call. He looked slightly sheepish, admitting that he had asked for her home address.

'Sorry, I'd forgotten all about it. I was merely curious. I wondered why you never speak of your home and always seemed so cagey about where you come from. You really needn't worry. I don't care if you come from the slums of the back of beyond. It's you that is important to me.

'You've obviously had a good education and seem to be fairly worldly. Put it down to my innate curiosity. Plain nosiness. Sorry if it's caused you any grief. I'll phone the wretched woman immediately and tell her that under no circumstances are you to be fired. OK?'

'I suppose so. But she did say that it was only a formality. I expect she interviews all her placements at some stage. There's nothing sinister about me, though. I promise. I just want you to know me for myself . . . without the baggage of a background.'

'But surely, it's one's background that helped form the person you are? Now, once and for all, whatever you're trying to hide, it doesn't matter to me. Don't you understand? Now come here.'

He pulled her towards him and gave her an entirely friendly, comforting hug. She resisted the urge to snuggle against him and tried to see his gesture for what it was.

Dom Discovers
The Truth

A week later, things were almost back to normal. The lounge floor, it turned out, needed only minimal repairs. A company was sent immediately and once powerful dehumidifiers had been put in place, things dried out well.

The garden seemed more of a problem, but Harris was allowed to employ a team of men to help restore it to some sort of order. The elderly man seemed to enjoy bossing everyone around and did very little actual work himself.

Lissa and Dom were beginning to form a close relationship, based on their growing friendship. They had spent some pleasant evenings together, often working on the computer game, which Lissa felt should never be counted as real work. They had now become comfortable with each other.

It was what Lissa wanted and she saw it could be a prelude for greater things to come and possibly, even some sort of future together. Even if it was only some wild dream in her imagination. When she was on her own, she held imaginary conversations with her father, telling him that this was truly the special man she had been waiting for. Always, the replies she imagined from her father were distinctly negative. She so often tried to make his replies become what she wanted to hear but it was to no avail.

She sensed that her father was never going to give his full approval to any man. She was on her own for once. She would have to make her own decisions. Dom, she acknowledged, was probably everything she could ever have dreamed of finding in a man.

The postponed luncheon parties had been arranged for the next day and Lissa worked hard with the prepara-tions. Some of the things she had made the previous week had been stored in the freezer so she was well organised. There would be ten guests, mostly old friends of Dom's father.

Ted Wetherill had left a letter requesting Dom to entertain his oldest friends to a meal, one last time as a more personal memorial. Dutifully, Dom had invited them all, to fulfil what he saw as an obligation to his father's memory.

Lissa had organised Mrs Rowley to give the dining room a spring clean and asked the unwilling Harris to see if he could find suitable flowers for the table and for a couple of displays. At least she was confident that she was able to arrange flowers reasonably well. It did, however, prove to be something of a problem after the events of the previous week.

The devastated garden was looking almost normal again and he had put in new plants and flowering shrubs. However, she suggested he might buy something suitable when he complained that he couldn't produce enough from the garden. Jane busied herself preparing the dishes and polishing glasses.

'This is just like the old days. Old Mr Wetherill always loved a luncheon party,' she said.

'I gather the guests will be pretty much from the old days, too. This is Dom's attempt to fulfil his father's wishes. I suppose this is the end of an era in some ways.'

'Well I think it's really lovely that he's taking such trouble.'

'I'm glad you approve,' Dom announced as he came into the room.

'I'm sorry, sir. You're always catching me out saying something I shouldn't.'

'Nonsense, Jane. And drop the 'sir' will you? Dom will do fine.' He spoke impatiently.

'Oh, I couldn't. Really I couldn't. I s'pose I could manage to call you Mr Dom, if that would do?'

'OK. If you must. Lissa, I wanted to ask you something. A favour. Would you please consider being my hostess at the lunch tomorrow? Makes the table more even and I'd be proud to have you helping to smooth things along. The woman's touch.'

'Thanks for asking, but I really couldn't. I'll have too much to do in the kitchen and besides, it would make things rather awkward. I'm sorry, Dom, but I have to say no.'

He was not at all pleased and spent several minutes trying to persuade her to change her mind. He even offered to hire a couple more girls from Mrs Jenkins, to act as waitresses but she remained adamant. She was being paid to cook and that was exactly what she intended to do.

She had it all worked out, especially as she had recognised some of the names on the guest list.

With any luck, she could remain in the kitchen and Jane would carry everything through to serve at the table. The meal she had planned should work beautifully.

Dom insisted on taking her out to

dinner, the evening before the lunch party.

'You've worked far too hard today to think about cooking tonight,' he told Lissa. Wearily, she agreed. It had been a long time since she had worked this hard . . . probably not since her original cookery course, she realised. Her tutor had been a real tyrant and an obsessed perfectionist.

'Good food deserves to be a work of pure science and served as a work of art,' he had always insisted. She would give it her best shot.

* * *

When they arrived at the restaurant, she gave a warning glance to the head waiter, as he was about to welcome her. He smiled discreetly, nodding his head knowingly. He was quite used to couples arriving in different combinations.

If Miss Langham wanted to be anonymous, that was fine with him. Her father was a very good customer and he'd hate to lose any trade. He must warn the other waiters not to recognise her.

'I'm sorry I'm not really doing justice to this lovely food,' Lissa apologised later. 'I guess I've seen so much food today, it's killed my appetite.'

'Don't worry. As long as there's nothing wrong with it.'

'Course not. It's all lovely. Very nice place this, isn't it?'

'Yes. I haven't been here before. You're sure everything is all right, isn't it?'

Lissa nodded.

'I'm still a bit concerned about Mrs Jenkins though. I still have to face her.'

'I did ring her again and said that you were highly satisfactory. She won't fire you, I promise.'

'She's a bit of an old battleaxe though. I'm not looking forward to seeing her again.'

'I shall keep you on anyhow, whatever she says. Even if I have to hide your car keys. Don't worry,' he ordered. 'I'm just sorry I ever said anything in the first place.'

They left the restaurant early. Lissa wanted a good night's sleep, in preparation for the following day. Dom went into his study and she could hear the click of his computer as she went to bed. Sleep did not come easily. She found herself thinking about her boss once more. If thinking about him all the time meant what people said it did, I really think I must love him, she realised with some surprise.

'I'm on my own this time, Daddy. For once I'm making my own decisions.'

★ ★ ★

Jane, in a smart black skirt and white shirt, kept for such occasions, welcomed the guests as they arrived. Drinks were served in the lounge and Dom excelled as a host. Most of the guests were elderly, apart from a couple of younger women, presumably daughters of old Mr Wetherill's friends. They spent much of the time flirting with Dom, who took it all with great charm. Jane kept Lissa informed of everything as it happened.

'There's one of them younger women absolutely throwing herself at Mr Dom. She's even swapped the place names so she can sit near to him. He's looking at her most uncomfortably. I'll let you know what happens next,' Jane giggled as she went back to collect more dishes.

Everything went very smoothly, according to Lissa's careful planning. The trays of food were waiting outside the dining room, ready for Jane to serve. Each course arrived promptly and seemed to be very well received by the group.

Lissa had caught sight of a couple of the guests, mutual friends of Dom's father as well as her own. Their eyes met and flickered with recognition.

She had suspected this might happen and had tried to keep right out of sight for the rest of the occasion. This had also been part of her reason for refusing to act as hostess. It would have completely blown her cover. She kept her fingers crossed that no-one would say anything to spoil her situation.

The doors to the garden were open and some of the party drifted on to the terrace for coffee. Lissa looked out of the window. Dom seemed to be deep in conversation with the couple she had recognised.

She hoped they were talking about books, remembering that this was a mutual interest. It was after four when the guests began to leave. Quite a lunch, she thought as she was clearing away the final dishes. Jane was exhausted.

'I'm sorry,' Lissa told her. 'I should have got someone else in to help you. It was too much for one person to do all that waiting at table. I really thought we'd manage.'

'It's OK. It was fine. You made it very easy for me. And everyone was very complimentary. I think you could get a job with several of them, if you wanted it.'

'Thanks. I think I'm quite happy where I am.'

'You like Mr Dom, don't you?'

'Course. Who wouldn't?'

'Really like him, I mean.'

'Well yes. I suppose I do.' She found herself blushing. Had her thoughts been quite so obvious?

'Just be careful, Lissa. I doubt he's going to stay here for very long. He doesn't really belong here. His home's always been in London. I'd hate for you to get hurt. You're really nice to work with.'

'Thanks, Jane. That's sweet of you to say so. But you needn't worry. I know what I'm doing.' She wished she felt as confident as her words. She knew her cheeks were redder than they should have been. If her thoughts were obvious to Jane, what must anyone else be thinking? She hoped she wasn't making a fool of herself.

She carried a tray of cutlery back to

the dining room to put away, not realising that the familiar couple were still talking to Dom. She quickly ducked behind the door, hoping again they had not seen her. When she heard the front door closing, she came out cautiously. Dom pounced on her.

'And why are you looking so furtive? Packing away the family silver, ready to steal it all later?'

'Dom, you made me jump. Is everything all right?'

'It's all wonderful, darling. You did a splendid job. Though I'm going to have to be careful or someone will steal you away from me. Several people were asking where I'd found a treasure like you.'

'Don't be silly.' She blushed partly at the compliment and partly because she realised he'd actually called her Darling. That was not a word to be taken lightly, not in her vocabulary.

'Truly, everyone was asking where I'd managed to find such a wonderful cook. They even wanted to meet you, to pass on their compliments. But I said you were very shy.' There was a wicked twinkle in his eye as he spoke and could barely stop grinning. 'We're going to have some champagne this evening. I feel like celebrating.'

Lissa stared.

'But why, Dom? I was only doing my job. The job you're paying me to do. But, all the same, champagne sounds wonderful.'

'And I insist on cooking dinner myself tonight. You have done enough for one day. Now, go and have a long soak in a hot bath. Relax. Pamper yourself. Any clearing that remains can be left until tomorrow.'

'But you have more guests the day after tomorrow. And there's still the dreaded Lettie Jenkins to face tomorrow afternoon,' she grimaced. 'I almost feel as if she was the spectre at the feast, watching everything I do to make sure it's perfectly correct.'

'Forget her. Forget everything. I promise you, tonight is for relaxing.'

* * *

Lissa lay in the bath, relaxing and looking forward to the bonus of the coming evening. It wasn't everyone whose boss treated her to champagne and as if she was someone special. She was such a lucky person. But her thoughts were scary. Loving someone this much was scary, if love it really was. She was just so inexperienced and without her father to guard her every move, she felt unsure of herself.

Suppose Dom didn't really love her back? She had known so few people who were really happily married or even had happy relationships. Her own mother had died far too early for her to know if they had loved each other. She wondered if her father had ever loved another woman.

Surely, he must have done. He was an attractive man and obviously rich enough to be a target for very many women. If that was the case, did he have the right to make such impositions on his daughter's choice of companion?

There was a knock on her door.

'Have you fallen asleep in there?' called Dom.

'Sorry. I was doing as I was told. Relaxing. I'll be right there.'

She quickly dried herself and brushed her hair. She twisted it into a knot on top of her head, leaving a few strands hanging loose. She had brought a few more of her better clothes from home on her last visit.

She put on one of her more expensive dresses. It was a deceptively simple sea-green silk, very cleverly cut. It clung to her slender figure like a second skin. She put on high, strappy sandals and clasped a slim gold chain round her neck. Playing the role of poverty stricken temp was over, at least for tonight.

'Wow,' Dom gasped as she walked slowly down the stairs. 'You look sensational. I wish my pathetic meal was going to be good enough for such a vision. Maybe we should go out somewhere after all.'

'Don't be silly,' Lissa said softly. 'Just being here with you is perfect. I felt I wanted to make an effort. To say thank you for being a lovely boss.'

'Wow,' Dom repeated. There may have been other women in his life, but this one, standing before him right now, was the one important thing in his life. He felt breathless at the sight of her and highly flattered that such a woman would go to these lengths for him.

Since he had actually learned from his lunch guests, exactly who she was, he had begun to feel slightly shy of her. Why hadn't he made the connection himself? Now he knew her real identity, everything had fallen into place. Langham. Lang Electronics. She'd also admitted she lived close and had obviously eaten in most of the expensive restaurants around.

Alistair Langham was her father. Dom's own computer was one of her father's products. No wonder the engineer had recognised her. They might even have been laughing behind his back. All the same, he thought he could understand why she had carried out her little deception. Perhaps she did simply want to prove herself.

He also understood why she was so anxious to know that he cared for her, without knowing who she really was. He could sympathise with her predicament. He'd often had women trying to get close to him, once they discovered who he was. He had himself, rejected a number of invitations when he thought they might be what his own father had referred to as gold-diggers.

He'd also become well aware of Alistair Langham's reputation where his only child was concerned. He'd heard that several men had been virtually paid-off to leave her alone. He understood all too well what it was like to be eligible, simply because of one's wealth or position.

Even at today's lunch, the two younger women members of the group had been flirting with him. They had been much too obvious and the one wretched woman had even changed the place names around. He'd especially organised that the wife of his father's greatest friend should sit next to him but to his irritation, that had been changed. He'd felt too embarrassed to make a fuss and had let it go.

All his life, he had never really known whether it was his money that seemed to make him attractive to women or whether it was merely their parents encouraging them by suggesting he was available. He pulled himself together as he stared at his companion.

'Sorry. I'm quite overwhelmed. You look like some exotic nymph from the sea. You're so lovely. But . . . come into the lounge. The champagne is ready and dinner, such as it is, is all ready to heat.'

Slightly nervous, Lissa went into the pretty lounge. The flowers, arranged for the lunch party, gave a delicate perfume to the air. Dom took her hand and led her to a large comfortable sofa. He crossed to the ice bucket and popped the cork from the champagne. He filled two crystal flutes and handed one to her.

'Can I dare to propose a toast? To us?'

'To us,' she replied softly. She felt nervous, awkward. Never before had she felt so uncertain of herself. She sipped the ice cold champagne and looked at Dom. He was wearing a light blue silk shirt that matched his eyes. His grey slacks fitted as if they had been made for him, which they probably had. She laughed at her silly thoughts.

'What are you smiling at?'

'I was just thinking that you look pretty good yourself. You were so busy complimenting me I scarcely looked at you.'

'I'm very pleased if you like what you see.'

'Oh I do. Indeed I do.'

Her voice felt shaky and she was trembling slightly. It wasn't every day that you admitted, if only to yourself, that you had fallen in love. She heard her father's voice somewhere in the distance telling her to be careful.

Go away, Daddy, she thought, I'm a big girl now and ready to make my own decisions.

Dom Decides To Test Lissa

They sipped their drinks, neither seeming to have much to say for once. They were both busy with their own thoughts. Lissa felt almost unable to speak as she was overcome with shyness. She still felt strangely apprehensive. After all her heart searching, it could turn out to be one huge mistake.

However complimentary Dom had been, was she making a fool of herself? Suppose he didn't feel the same way about her? She must be careful or she could get hurt. Even Jane had mentioned that she should be careful. This was not Dom's natural habitat. He was a city man. 'I was . . . '

'Would you . . . ' they both said exactly together.

'Sorry, you first . . . ' again, they

spoke together. They both laughed nervously.

'Look, there's something I need to tell you,' Dom began. He looked serious.

'From the look on your face, I don't think I'm going to want to hear it. Let's just enjoy dinner and then maybe we can have another go at your amazing computer game? No talking about anything important. Let's just enjoy a nice companionable evening with nothing to cause any upset.'

Her mind was whirling. Obviously, she'd made some sort of huge mistake and he was about to sack her. Or maybe it was something much worse and she didn't want to spoil this moment. Nothing should spoil their evening now.

Dom frowned. He had been on the verge of telling her that he knew who she was. The frown left his face and he grinned, thinking that he might even enjoy his own little deception.

He believed he could understand why she was making this stand. He had once been through a similar situation with his own father. Following his education at a well-known public school and finishing a university education at one of the most historic and prestigious, he'd spent a year wandering around Europe.

'You've been too used to being pampered all your life,' his father had told him. 'You don't know what it is to have to earn a living. I suggest you go and get some sort of a job and you might learn how the rest of the world copes.'

Dom remembered the bitter feelings he'd had at the time and how deeply he had resented the comments. After all, he'd obtained a very good degree and that had entailed a great deal of work and ability. Admittedly, with some financial assistance from his father, he had started his own business and it had grown rapidly until he was now financially secure and making decent profits. Maybe she had gone through something similar with her own father.

'There's some champagne left, if you'd like it. And then we ought to consider dinner.'

'I'm not sure I've got a lot of room for dinner, after the lunch. Jane and I had some of the leftovers. More champagne would be nice though.'

'It's my cooking you're scared of, isn't it? Admit it.'

'Depends what you're planning. Or have you already prepared something?'

'I was going to make scrambled eggs with smoked salmon. Virtually my only speciality.'

'Sounds perfect. Just right. Any man who can make decent scrambled eggs, can't be all bad.'

'You haven't tasted them yet. Shall we have trays in here? You look weary. Stay there and I'll bring supper to you.'

'Thank you. I do suddenly feel tired. Must be the wine.' He grinned as he left her lying back against his father's large comfortable cushions on the elderly sofa. She closed her eyes and drifted off into a deep sleep and didn't stir even when Dom came back into the room carrying a large tray.

He stared at her. Dear, sweet Lissa. She looked so childlike and innocent. Vulnerable, even. Strange, considering the life she must have led. Most people had heard of her father and his shrewd, tough business methods.

His only daughter had been kept out of the limelight for most of her life but the rumours had persisted. She must have found her role as housekeeper extremely difficult. She must always have had someone to look after her every need. And here she was, pretending to be his housekeeper. He gave a small grin. Perhaps he might enjoy testing her . . . good-naturedly teasing her, over the next few days.

He would find out just how capable she really was in her self-imposed role, acting as housekeeper. His smile faded as he thought longer term. He didn't want to spoil anything at all . . . any possibilities for a future with this woman.

Though he felt confident that they were both developing feelings for each other that were genuine, he was concerned that Alistair Langham was not going to be too pleased. In fact, her father was probably capable of arranging for some event to remove Dom from the scene altogether, if he disapproved of a relationship between him and his daughter.

'Hey, you. Wake up. Supper time. Here you are, sleeping soundly while I've been slaving away in the kitchen. Can't think what I'm paying you for.'

'Oh, Dom. I'm so sorry. I couldn't keep my eyes open. Can I help?'

'It's all right. I'm just teasing. Sit up.' He put the tray down on the coffee table and handed her a plate and a fork. 'This should be manageable on your knee. Toast is here.'

The plate was piled with a light mound of scrambled egg and pieces of smoked salmon criss-crossed over it. Dom had cut buttered toast into triangles and placed them within easy reach. He topped up her champagne glass and settled himself beside her.

'This is really good,' she said as she tucked in. 'Didn't think I felt hungry until I saw it.' She took a final piece of toast and wiped the plate clean and gave a contented sigh. 'You're the sort of boss anyone would die for. Feeds me wonderful food and champagne and entertains me royally.'

'I suppose that as a boss, I should have been giving you time off. I suddenly feel guilty. You haven't had a day off since you arrived and it's weeks now. Once we've had the next lunch party, you must have a day or two to yourself. Lettie Jenkins will be suing me for exploitation if I'm not careful. Promise me you won't tell her?'

'Just don't mention that woman's name again. Don't spoil a lovely evening.'

★ ★ ★

It was a relaxed evening and the pair chatted about their childhood and schools and trivia that makes the beginnings of any relationship. Lissa took great care not to give herself away and though she admitted being at boarding school, was at pains not to mention the actual name of what was one of the more prestigious establishments, the cost of which was way out of most people's league. She felt too relaxed to be involved with his computer games for the evening, it was soon bedtime.

'Have a good sleep,' Dom ordered, 'and don't worry about breakfast in the morning. I'll grab what I want and probably start work. Have a lie in if you want to. You'll be busy enough later getting ready for the next invasion of lunch guests. I'm sure Dad would have been delighted with the way things are going and I feel I've done justice to his wishes.'

Lissa fell into bed and slept soundly. She heard nothing and woke with a start as the sun streamed into her room. It was late. Jane and Mrs Rowley would be here within the next half-hour. She shot out of bed and dressed quickly. She would shower later once everyone was organised. There was a smell of coffee lingering in the air.

Dom must have had his breakfast and was presumably working in his study. She put on a fresh pot, shoved bread into the toaster and went to look for her boss. She tapped on the study door and then drew back as she heard him on the phone. She went back to the kitchen and sat down to eat her breakfast. She had scarcely finished when Jane arrived.

'You're late this morning. Sleep in, did you?'

'Yes, I did. Must have been more tired than I realised. I think Dom must have helped himself to breakfast. He was on the phone so I didn't disturb him.'

'Talking about me?' Dom asked as he came into the room. The two girls smiled as they nodded together.

'I was just saying that I hoped you'd

had some breakfast.'

'Yes thanks. No problem. I'm going to be busy this morning. Papers to sort out. Then I have a meeting later this afternoon with the solicitors for Dad's estate. Could you give my grey suit a sponge and press? Do whatever you have to do to make it presentable. Thanks.'

She didn't see his slightly teasing smile as he turned from the table. He thought she probably wouldn't have a clue about such things.

'Er yes. Of course, Sir.'

'You never called me sir in your life,' he said with a grin. 'But I would like the suit ready before lunch if you can manage it. And my black shoes need a clean. I walked through something disgusting last time out.'

Lissa gulped. Press and sponge a suit? How on earth did one do that? Did housekeepers do that sort of thing? There couldn't be much to it. She could probably just about manage to iron a shirt but pressing something?

Was there any difference? Maybe she needed to phone Mrs Bates. She'd be sure to know.

Some time later, she was fighting with the ironing board. Surely the thing was supposed to stay up when you lifted it? Jane came into the room.

'There's a little catch thing underneath. Always a bit tricky.'

Lissa nodded her thanks, feeling slightly stupid. She plugged in the iron and waited for it to heat. What had Mrs Bates said? Use a damp tea-cloth. She picked up the dishcloth and eyed it. It looked a little grubby but it would probably be all right. She rinsed it out and laid it carefully over the trouser leg. She picked up the iron and rested it on the cloth.

The hiss of steam was quite dramatic. A greasy stain spread over the trousers and bits of white fluff from the cloth imprinted themselves into the fabric. Lissa stared in horror.

'Jane,' she called. 'Can you come here please?'

She stood with the mess in front of her and waited. Jane looked and smiled.

'Oh dear. You should have used a tea towel not a dish cloth. And I think maybe the iron's a bit too hot.'

'I didn't know there was a difference. Mrs B said . . . I mean I knew I needed to use a tea cloth. I didn't think it would matter which particular cloth I used.'

Jane stared at her and wisely said nothing. 'I think the trousers just became a job for the dry cleaners. Trouble is, there isn't time. He wants them this afternoon.'

'Why don't we say the suit is too bad for you to do? It needs proper cleaning. You could drop it round to them later. See if there's something else he can wear. I'm sure that can't be his only available suit.'

Dom was not best pleased when she went into the study to tell him. She felt near to tears, mostly of frustration. It wasn't the suit. He'd only meant to tease Lissa a little, not to upset her.

Give her her due, she hadn't

admitted anything and maybe the suit did need a proper clean anyway. He needed to take care just how much he did tease her, if he was to achieve everything he hoped for a future with her.

'And my shoes?' he asked.

'Oh, crumbs. I completely forgot the shoes.'

He gave a sigh and a slight shrug as he turned away to hide his smile.

'I'm sorry, I quite forgot to say. Two of the ladies who had been invited but couldn't come to lunch yesterday, called to ask if they might call in today. I did say we'd give them something for lunch. Just a light lunch. Nothing elaborate. Something and salad? Is that OK?'

'Of course,' Lissa replied quickly, still smarting from the possible ruination of his suit and wanted a way to make it up to him. She thought quickly about what was in the freezer and knew there were things she could use. 'One o'clock be all right?'

'Perfect. Oh and I would like you to sit down with us. It will all be very informal and I'm sure you'll ease things. No need for Jane to be a waitress today. Save her strength for tomorrow. Right then. They will be here about twelve-thirty if you can let them in, Jane.'

They had a busy morning, quickly putting together a lunch, with Jane setting the table. Her disaster with the suit gradually fading in her mind as she concentrated on a starter with smoked salmon, left over from their meal last night and a hurriedly made quiche and salad. For pudding, she was serving strawberries and ice cream.

Well, Dom had said keep it simple. She still had work to do for the next lunch party on the following day. Once that was over, there was just the one small dinner party before the diary was empty for a while.

Maybe she would get the promised day off, though what she would do with it, she was unsure. Maybe the whole job was nearing its end, as he concluded his business here. Perhaps he would decide to sell up and return to London. Every sensible part of her was telling her not to get involved. Not to become even more fond of Dom. But her heart continued to beat harder at the very thought of him.

The simple lunch for the two elderly ladies, who were more of the old friends of his father, went well. They had been unable to attend the previous day's gathering so Dom had felt it was necessary to arrange this second lunch on the spur of the moment.

He was unsure of the actual connection with his father, but it had been something to do with the book collection. His sense of duty made him carry out his father's wishes and he smiled resignedly. He was relieved that on this occasion, Lissa had agreed to act as his hostess.

For her part, she felt nothing mattered any more. If they were mutual friends of her own father, so be it. She knew she had to confess everything to Dom and confess it very soon.

Jane helped with the serving after all, but Lissa left the table between the courses to ensure that all the food was as perfect as possible. She returned to find Dom looking slightly uncomfortable at the intense interrogation he'd been suffering.

Who was she? Was there something between them? What a lovely couple they made.

How much his father would have liked her. He tried hard to fend off their suggestive comments, not wanting them to embarrass Lissa. They did at least change the subject when she came back into the room, much to Dom's relief.

Eventually, they were ready to go and collected handbags and coats. Lissa turned to finish clearing the table and one of the ladies came back.

'You do make such a nice couple. Ted would have been so proud to have you join his family. Look after him, won't you dear?'

Lissa stood gaping, trying to collect her thoughts. What on earth had Dom said to them? She felt slightly shocked.

'I'm not sure what you're saying,' she stammered. 'I'm Dom's housekeeper. That's all.'

'You may try to pretend that's all it is, my dear. But when you get to my age, you learn to look out for the signs. It's blatantly obvious you're in love with each other. The little glances. Delightful to see. Be happy. And thank you for a wonderful meal. Goodbye.'

She went out to her companion and with a definite twinkle in her eye, she kissed Dom and left with a little wave.

'I simply don't know what all that was about,' she said, repeating the old lady's comments as they went back into the house.'

'I promise, I said nothing,' Dom insisted.

'Evidently we don't need to say anything for some people to begin their speculations.'

'Evidently not.' He looked troubled.

Lissa was a sensitive person and was clearly disturbed at any suggestion of a relationship. He smiled, pulled himself together and said, 'Now, I must get off to my meeting.'

Lissa cleared up the remaining lunch things and finished her preparations for the following day. It was almost five o'clock by the time she felt she could even think about relaxing for the rest of the day. Just as she had sat down with a cup of tea, the phone rang. She answered it to hear a furious Lettie Jenkins demanding to know where she was. She had completely forgotten the meeting she was supposed to attend. Her heart sank.

'I'm really sorry. I'll drive over right away. I was rather busy here with Dom, erm, Mr Wetherill needing me to serve a lunch party. It was all rather unexpected and I'm afraid my appointment with you completely slipped my mind.'

★ ★ ★

When she arrived at the agency office, Lettie was brusque to say the least. Lissa was tempted to tell her to get lost, but she would have played into her father's hands, indirectly. It would undoubtedly have proved she could not keep a job and trivial though it might seem, that had become a matter of pride.

'I am not used to having a single one of my recommendations cause me problems in any way,' she finished her tirade.

'But what on earth did Mr Wetherill say?' Lissa asked curiously.

'Well, he asked about your background. Where you'd been previously. Where you were trained. Your home address. All perfectly reasonable and, reading between the lines, I had to ask myself, were you entirely suitable for this job. Now you begin to see why I was troubled. There's the security for one thing. I gather there are some very valuable items at Templars. I bitterly regret not being more thorough in taking up your references. It was almost an emergency situation at the time and I didn't do a proper follow up, as I usually do.'

'But Mr Wetherill seemed more than happy with my work,' she remarked, her tongue firmly in her cheek.

'Oh, I gather he is happy enough. But it's the fact that you are underqualified for the job specified. That really troubles me. My reputation is at stake. I feel I should have found a properly qualified person. One with housekeeper training not just a cook. It reflects on my own professionalism.'

'But if he wants me to stay, surely that's all that matters? Dom said himself, that he doesn't want to replace me. That he's completely satisfied with me.'

'Dom?' she questioned, eyebrows virtually disappearing into her hairline in shocked surprise.

'Mr Wetherill. He asked me to call him Dom. Short for Dominic. He dislikes formality.'

'I see. Not quite like the old days, I gather. I had Miss Elsie Smythe in here the other day. His ex-housekeeper. She has such excellent qualifications. Very high standards and impeccably organised. If the young Mr Wetherill wants informality, I suppose that must give a clue as to why she left him. The reason she felt unable to continue in the role she had held for very many years with old Mr Wetherill. It's just not the thing, this informality. Familiarity with the staff does not make for a smoothly run household. Perhaps I should have been more particular in taking him on to my list in the first place. Oh and as to your home address, I simply don't have one listed for you.'

'I'm sort of between addresses. As I'm living in, I hadn't bothered to find anywhere more permanent yet.' The lies slipped out very easily, she realised. It was becoming quite a habit.

'Well, Miss Langham. I'm giving you a formal warning about your conduct. If there are any further problems, I'm afraid I shall have to remove you from our books. I'm sorry, but there it is.'

'Very well. Thank you. I'm not exactly sure why my conduct is in question. But, I'll try to do my best to please Mr Wetherill.'

She shook hands with the dour lady and left, laughing so much inside that she found it hard to keep her face composed. Such antiquated ideas and a level of formality. She had standards that belonged to pre-war days for at least minor royalty, for both her staff and clients.

★ ★ ★

Much later in the evening, when she gave her account of the meeting to Dom, he found it highly entertaining.

'My name will be mud, no doubt. I'll never be able to use the agency again.'

'Why would you? Aren't you going to keep me on as your employee?'

'I'll decide later. Though I'm not sure about your long term role as my employee. I don't seriously think it's what you want as a career. I suspect you will soon be tired of this place and the work involved. Bit too menial for someone like you.'

'Certainly not, sir. I'll always do my best, sir.'

She said it with a servant girl demeanour and almost touching her forelock as she gave a slight bob of a curtsey. He gave a roar of laughter.

'You're funny. I doubt I've ever met anyone less like a housekeeper than you are. Maybe what I'm trying to say is that I don't actually want you to go on being my housekeeper.

'Ultimately, I hope that you will have a different role in my life.'

He was staring at her with an intensity she found disturbing. She felt her cheeks colouring and burning. A different role? Surely he couldn't mean what she was hoping he meant?

She almost dared not think of it. He stared back, trying to gauge what she was thinking. It wasn't something he took lightly at this moment, it was a forever thing. Perhaps, she thought, it was the right time to confess her deception.

'There's something I should tell you,' Lissa began.

'I know. I know, Lissa. It's all right.'

'But you can't know what I was going to tell you.'

'I think I do.'

She had been going to tell him about her father. She had been on the edge of telling him the truth but he had stopped her. She wondered what he'd been expecting her to say. Perhaps it was for the best to remain silent for a little longer. She really needed to be patient.

Dom, had also reached a decision. He recognised that this was something much more that he may ever have intended. He was attracted to this woman . . . no, he was besotted by her, infatuated, even in love. He wanted to tell her . . . tell the world. Somehow, he needed to tell her, to share his feelings before letting on that he knew who she was.

She might not believe his feelings were genuine, though with his own background and continued careful management, money would never be any sort of problem.

'I'm going to have an early night. I'm sure you're tired too and it's another busy day for you tomorrow. After this little round, we shall have a few quiet days. In fact, I'm going to have to be away for a few days. I need to go and sort out some business in London. You can take a few days off. Don't worry, it will be in lieu of the days you haven't taken. I shall still pay you of course.'

'That's OK. No worries. I shall miss you,' she added, almost shyly.

They went their separate ways. She took some things from the freezer to defrost and he went to his study. There was a tension between them neither able to voice their thoughts and neither quite daring to believe in an outcome they would both want.

The lunch party the following day was another success. It was easier then the previous one as Lissa and Jane had formed an excellent working pattern. On this occasion, there were no people present that Lissa knew so she was more relaxed.

The following day, Dom packed a bag and drove away during the morning. She planned to do a bit of cooking to stock the freezer, make sure everything was clean and tidy and then she would go back home for a day or two.

She even considered trying to contact her father to make things right between them. In her flurry of activity and meeting Dom, it had rather been pushed to the back of her mind.

The two stubborn people, so alike, had to make up their minds to be friends again. Their argument had all been so silly and so trivial.

Her plans were doomed to failure,

however. She went back to her own home feeling certain there would be some news of her father. Bates and his wife had neither seen nor heard anything of him. Mrs Bates was delighted to see 'her baby' back and made a great fuss of her.

The old lady sensed a new independence in her girl. She had a different attitude to everything and thanked her often for the little things she did.

'That's fine, my dear. Nice you think to say, thank you, though. Much appreciated. Your time away seems to have had an effect on you. Glad to see it. Is your job finished now?'

'Certainly not. I'm just having a couple of days off. I'm wondering where Daddy is. It's not like him to disappear so completely. Maybe I should phone his office again. See what they know.'

She did so, but it was a fruitless exercise. His secretary said he was somewhere in the States and had not left a number. His personal assistant was looking after everything and Mr Langham had said nothing about his immediate plans and certainly made no mention of his return.

'Luckily, we're not busy at present and there's nothing urgent needing his attention,' the personal assistant had told her.

Lissa drifted around the house for a couple of days and drove to Milton Keynes to do some shopping on another day. She bought a few clothes and sat in a cafe overlooking the main hall of the shopping centre. Watching people milling round, all intent and seemingly full of purpose with what they were doing made her realise just how empty her own life has been.

She was missing Dom. Ridiculous. She had only known him for a few weeks so how could she seriously be missing him? She would have liked him to say he cared for her, just a little bit, before she confessed the truth about her real identity.

She was certain he did have feelings

for her. If he said he cared when he knew who she was, she might wonder if it was because of that or if it was truly genuine. Her father had certainly done quite a job in destroying her self-confidence.

She finished her coffee and drove the few miles back to her home. One more day and she could take it no longer. She went back to Templars, Dom's lovely old house. It still wasn't quite as lovely as their own place but it offered so much more. She could be in charge of something there. Be occupied. And furthermore, Dom might be coming back soon. She wanted to be there the moment he arrived back, ready to greet him.

Dom Contacts Alistair

It was another two days before Dom arrived back. No phone calls and nothing to herald his arrival. Lissa and Jane were sitting in the kitchen having a gossip over a cup of tea before Jane left for the day, when they heard a car stop on the gravel drive.

'Are we expecting anything or anyone?' Lissa asked.

'Not that I know of. I'll go and see who it is.' Seconds later, she bounced back into the kitchen. 'Guess who's back? Good job we spring cleaned his room and got everything ship shape.'

Lissa felt her heart racing. She blushed and quickly finger combed her hair. Too late to smarten herself properly but at least she was wearing decent jeans and one of her new T-shirts. She put the dirty mugs into the dishwasher and went to greet the man who had become so special in her life.

'Hi there,' she said as calmly as she could. 'Good trip?'

'Not bad. London's too crowded and too busy. I've got used to the quiet of the country. I think I should have made a couple of train journeys instead of staying up there. All is sorted for a while anyhow. What's been going on here?'

'Nothing much. I did have a few days off anyway, remember? Do you want a coffee?'

'Yes, why not. I'll bring my stuff in after that. I feel shattered.'

Jane had made a speedy exit, not wanting to be delayed by Dom's return home. It was already well after her usual time but she had been enjoying the gossip.

'It's Dom back home, Jane,' Lissa began but paused when she saw the kitchen was empty. She felt ridiculously pleased that she didn't have to share his return with anyone.

She made coffee for them both and sat at the kitchen table. She felt suddenly shy and didn't know what to say. He smiled hesitantly, clearly facing the same problem.

'I showed everyone the new game with the modifications you had suggested.'

'I wasn't aware that I had made any suggestions.'

'Well, subconsciously maybe. It was probably more things I noticed weren't working properly. I need to spend some time on it though and I'd be grateful for your input again. It's a case of someone who isn't computer literate having a play with the game and discovering what doesn't gel and what could be done to improve it.'

'Sounds great. I've missed playing while you were away.'

'I'd hoped you might have missed me too. Just a little.'

'Of course I did. There was nobody to cook for,' she teased.

'That's all about to change again.

What's for dinner tonight?'

'What do you want? Considering we had no idea you were coming back, I haven't prepared anything at all.'

'Something fishy would be good. Have you got any salmon?'

She nodded and went to search the freezer. She would make her special salmon and pasta dish with vegetables and asparagus sauce. It was always her father's favourite when they occasionally dined together at home.

When she went back into the kitchen, Dom had disappeared. She heard him moving around upstairs and assumed he was unpacking. She hummed to herself as she prepared the food, ready to be heated later.

The dish used a mix of different ingredients that could be kept in stock so it was all very easy. With a cold bottle of something dry and white, she was sure to impress.

'Mmm, something smells good. I suspect we need a cold white to go with it?'

'We?'

'You know how much I hate eating alone.'

'I doubt Lettie Jenkins would approve of such informality. I'm still smarting from her comments. Us servants should know our place.'

'Lissa, Lissa. Come here. How can you think you're a servant of any sort?' He held out his hands to her and slowly she came towards him. He put his arms round her and held her close. He bent to kiss her closed eyes and then released one arm to tilt her chin towards his mouth. She relaxed against him and felt herself floating somewhere above the ground. It was dangerous territory.

'I need to stir the sauce or something,' she stammered, scared that she might be totally out of control if he kissed her again.

'I'm sorry. I've been missing you. London was awful without you. But it felt good to know I had you to come home to.' He looked at her flushed face and the confusion in her eyes and clenched his lips together. 'I'm sorry, Lissa. I forgot myself for a moment. Please forgive me. I'll go and take a quick shower and then we can eat. Won't be long.'

He rushed out of the room and up the stairs. Lissa took several deep breaths, trying her best to get control of herself. She felt as if her knees might let her down at any moment and her mind was somewhere in what might have been paradise.

Concentrating hard, she poured boiling water over the pasta and stood looking at it on the unheated cooker. Ten minutes later, Dom came back into the room. She was still staring at the pan with uncooked pasta in it.

'You ready? Or should I go away again?' he asked.

'No, no. Stay. It's almost ready. I'll just boil up the pasta. Didn't want to overcook it.' She pulled herself together and concentrated on the meal. He watched her as she deftly stirred the sauce and mixed colourful ingredients.

'Shall I open the wine? I've chosen a New Zealand Sauvignon Blanc. I hope that will do?'

'Perfect. Not too heavy and usually flavoursome.'

'You know your wines. Nice to have someone who appreciates the differences. Can't stand women who say they'll drink anything.'

They sat down and he helped himself to a large portion. 'Wow, this is fantastic. Is this someone famous' recipe? These celebrity chefs all produce different speciality things.'

'It's one of my own inventions. A happy accident. I made it with some leftovers once when I was unexpectedly cooking for my father.'

'You don't usually cook for your father?'

'Not often.' She paused, not wanting to give anything else away. 'Will you have some more?'

'Certainly will. Don't know how you managed such an amazing meal at short notice.'

'It's actually quite quick to do. Some more parmesan?'

He took the grated cheese and ate heartily. He topped up her glass and touched her hand.

'I'm sorry about kissing you. I hope you're not too angry with me.'

She shook her head, her cheeks colouring again.

''Course not. It was a bit unexpected.'

'Good. I'd hate to cause you any sort of upset.'

'I haven't made any sort of pudding. Would you like some ice-cream.'

'I don't think so. I made a pig of myself with the main course. Shall we have coffee in the study? I'm anxious to try out my computer game on you, now it's been modified.'

'OK. I'll just load the dishwasher and be with you when the coffee's ready.'

It was safer ground. Once he was involved in his games, it was unlikely to lead to anything she felt unable to cope with. Whatever she thought of her newly found independence, her father did have a point. She should behave with great care until she was absolutely certain she was doing the right thing.

She wished more than ever that she could just have a talk to her father. It was ridiculous feeling like this. They were much too close to each other to be apart for so long, especially under the cloud of anger they had both created.

Dom was staring at his screen, much as Lissa had stared at the pan of pasta. His mind was racing. Somehow, he had to resolve his dilemma. He had fallen in love with her and felt certain she shared his feelings. The kiss had told him what he wanted to know . . . that his feelings were mutual. He'd known her identity for too long now and it was impossible to say anything that she might believe.

He knew that he needed to face the lion in its lair. He would see her father and formally ask for his daughter's hand in marriage. He was suitably old-fashioned to want to do it properly and knew that it had to be the best approach for someone like Alistair Langham.

He gave a smile of recognition as a workable plan was forming. He would invite him to dinner. The slight irony of getting the man's own daughter to cook for him was also slightly amusing, to say the least. He would say nothing to Lissa until after her father arrived and he had the chance to make his formal request.

She came into the study with the coffee tray and they settled down to wander into the mysterious world of Narl, his own creation.

★   ★   ★

Dom phoned Mr Langham the following morning. He had previously called the London office and was told by a secretary that he was unavailable. However, a message was left, along with the invitation to dinner. It took only a short time for the reply to arrive. Luckily, Dom answered the phone himself, otherwise he would have been totally caught out in his schemes, should Lissa have answered.

'Ted, my old friend,' Alistair Langham said, as Dom spoke.

'Mr Langham? This is Ted's son, Dominic. I'm so sorry. You obviously haven't heard. My father died about two months ago.'

There was a gasp of horror from the other end.

'Why wasn't I told before now?'

'Everything happened so suddenly. I had to make all the funeral arrangements immediately. Though I put announcements in the better papers, it wasn't until some time later I began to go through my father's diaries and records, I discovered a number of people who ought to have been told personally. I have been working through the list and I apologise that I left it so late in finding you.'

'I've been away. Only got back at some ungodly hour this morning. Your call was the first I looked at.'

The next few exchanges were predictably painful for Dom. Describing the cause of his father's death and all that had happened since, were still difficult. Alistair was devastated that he'd been unaware of any of it, including the funeral.

'I've been trying to make up and I'm gradually contacting my father's oldest friends. I'd like to talk to you about something. I wondered if you'd be free to have dinner with me one evening?'

'Of course, dear boy. Delighted. As it happens, I'm free Saturday, if that's any good? After that, I shall be away again for some time.'

'Excellent. Saturday's fine. I'd be pleased if you would join me here at Templars. Around seven-thirty then?'

'I expect you'll be wanting some advice about your father's books.'

'Among other things. I'm actually thinking of selling some of them.'

Alistair's reaction was predictable.

'Ah, right. And I expect you are going

to offer me first refusal. Very proper, I must say.'

'Perhaps we can talk about all of that when we meet, sir?' Dom said, anxious to end the conversation before something was said that shouldn't have been.

'I shall look forward to it. I always enjoy Elsie Smythe's cooking. Thank you for the invitation. Goodbye.' He hung up before Dom could say anything more.

After the call, he began to have serious doubts about his plans and he said nothing about the change of housekeeper. How could he have done so without letting any cats out of the bag? Suppose Lissa was upset? She might even be furiously angry that he had been so devious and there was no way he could pretend it had all been an accident.

Heavens, he still scarcely knew her and predicting how she might react was entering the unknown. Here he was, making plans to ask her father if he might marry and settle down with her without even asking her first. But in his heart, he was certain that it was everything he had been waiting for . . . all his life. He had only to think of her, her lovely face and her interesting mind. He truly wanted her. He rose from his desk and went in search of her.

'Lissa? Where are you?' he called loudly, when she wasn't in the kitchen. He still wasn't totally sure why she had taken this job. Surely there were other ways of discovering herself, if that was indeed what she was trying to do?

Dom glanced through the window, into the garden. Careful management and restoration had placed the garden back to its place among the sights of the area. Harris the gardener and his team had done an excellent job, even if the cost was somewhat off the planet. Dom owed it to his father's memory.

His heart leapt as he saw Lissa, setting his pulse racing with a passion he could barely control. The image of her seemed to haunt him whatever he was doing.

At this moment she was a vision, set among the pink roses. She was cutting the flowers, snipping away deadheads as she picked the fresh blooms. He knew that he truly loved her. She looked up as if sensing his presence. He waved and she dropped the flowers into a basket hanging on her arm and came inside.

'You look like the perfect country maiden. Come here.' He took her hands, her soft, slender hands and pressed them against his chest. 'Darling girl. I just needed to hold you for a moment. I'm afraid I've become very fond of you.' He bent his head to kiss her and she responded willingly.

'Suppose Jane comes in?'

'So what? I'm not going to kiss her as well.'

'Idiot,' she laughed. 'I just don't want to embarrass her.'

She was delighted and overwhelmed with joy. He had said he was fond of her. Very fond of her. This wonderful man had actually said he cared about her without knowing who she was. For herself and not because she had a wealthy father. She stood on tiptoe and kissed him, knowing that she wanted this euphoria to go on forever. 'Did you actually call me for something?' she asked.

'Just to say I have another business friend coming to dinner Saturday evening. I hope that isn't a problem?'

'Of course not. That's what I'm here for. And there's someone else on Friday evening, isn't there?' She'd noticed that he'd written the long postponed arrangements in her kitchen diary.

'I'm afraid so. Am I working you too hard? Sorry, but I wanted to get all this out of the way as soon as possible. I promise, after this, there will be very little extra to do. I shall look forward to having you to myself again.'

'Anything special you'd like for Friday and Saturday, come to that? In the way of food for the various dinners.'

'I suspect tomorrow's lot are vegetarian. But that will be in Elsie's little black book, I expect.'

'You won't mind having veggie for once?'

'Course not. I do actually like vegetarian dishes.'

'And for Saturday? How many guests?'

'Just one. I leave the menu to you. Something to go with claret, I think. I seem to remember he is particularly fond of claret.' He smiled to himself at his cleverness. Hadn't she said that her father was fond of that particular claret they'd shared on her first night here?

'Right. Leave it with me.'

'Thanks. And to make up, I'll take you somewhere special tonight.'

'You don't have to. I enjoy cooking. This is my job, after all.'

'But I want to. I want to be seen with you. You're a very beautiful lady and I want to show you off.'

It seemed this was the start of some

new arrangement in their relationship. It would take some getting used to. Perhaps now was the time she should come clean. She didn't quite know how she was expected to behave and felt slightly ill at ease, despite the feeling that she was going to burst with happiness.

★   ★   ★

They drove out to a small country pub which had a good reputation for food. When they arrived they discovered there was a live group playing. The whole place was packed and Dom immediately suggested they should find somewhere else to eat.

'Let's listen for a bit while we have a drink. We don't always have to go to quiet places with posh food.' He gave a shrug and found a small space on a bench near to several other people.

'They're good, aren't they?' she asked Dom.

'Yes . . . not bad. Bit noisy though.

We can't exactly talk much,' he almost shouted.

'We always talk.'

'Not just talk. There are things we need to discuss. Personal stuff.'

'Sorry?'

'Let's move on,' Dom begged. He was not used to feeling quite so embarrassed. 'I know another little pub that I doubt will be so busy. Come on.' He took her hand and steered her through the throng. The group were beginning another number and the noise was starting to build again.

'You're right. It's a bit noisy for comfort. Heavens, I must be getting old. I always loved live music.'

They drove away and she suddenly realised where they were. They were going to drive right past her own home. She felt the colour rise in her cheeks as they approached and hoped that no-one was looking out from the house, as they passed.

Ridiculous, she told herself. Even if anyone was looking out, they were hardly going to recognise her in a strange car. She couldn't help but stare down the drive. She gave a jolt as she saw her father's car standing in front of the door. She let out her breath, unaware that she'd been holding it.

She hadn't checked her mobile in several days. Maybe her father had left a message by now. She wondered what on earth she was going to say to him when finally, they did meet.

This had been the longest spell apart they'd ever had, without calls or messages of any kind. If the two old ladies had seen something between her and Dom, surely her father would guess something as well. After all, he did claim to know her every mood. At least it would come as a surprise to Dom when he discovered her identity. He may even feel gratified to realise that she wasn't at all interested in his money.

'Anything wrong?' Dom asked, quite unaware that this was her own home territory.

'No. Nothing. I was miles away.' But her mind was filled with the thought that her father was back. He must know by now what she was doing. Bates would have told him that she was working. She actually had a job.

She almost wished she could have been there to see his face. She wondered what she should do. She desperately wanted to make up with her father but he had to see that he had been most unfair. Knowing him the way she did, she doubted he would ever acknowledge that he might be wrong. Alistair Langham was never, ever, wrong.

'I think it's just down here,' Dom said as he turned off the main road.

'Yes. It is. If it's the Jugglers you're looking for.'

'Is there anywhere round here you haven't been to?' he asked good-naturedly.

'I suppose not. I've sort of lived around here most of my life.'

'Is it a problem?'

'Not at all. But they do know me,'

she said slowly. Might they give away her identity, she wondered?

Suddenly she felt weary of the whole business. What did it matter? She'd been on the brink anyway, of telling Dom the truth last night. 'No, it's fine. Let's go in. They do a mean chilli here.'

'Right. Let's sample your chilli then.'

Almost for the first time since she'd known Dom, she felt relaxed when they were out, not worrying about being recognised by the restaurant staff. They'd travelled too far now, for it to matter what people thought. She no longer felt duty bound to keep her secret, though she still hoped to tell him in her own time.

'Nice to see you, Lissa,' said the barman. She'd been here with Tony Mason on more than one occasion and knew that the man would say nothing to embarrass her. He must be used to people coming in with different partners from time to time.

He kept staring at Dom, however and Lissa realised that probably, he was aware of what her father had said to Tony. That particular man had come out of it all right. Her father had given him a generous cheque to leave her alone. She knew, because that was exactly what her father had told her, when they'd had their monumental row.

'You're right. This chilli's certainly very good,' Dom said, his mouth full of the delicious spicy meat. 'I'm going to need something long and cold after this. You seem preoccupied. I hope you're OK?'

'Course. I was just thinking about what to cook tomorrow.'

'Leave your work behind you.'

'You certainly seem to have done. How does your company manage without you for so long?'

'I've been working all the time. I don't just sit in my study playing games, you know. I use the Internet. Keep in touch with the office via email. All the same, I will have to go to London next week. Just for a few days. Things I need to sort out. Maybe you could come too? Do some shopping or whatever you like to do in London. It might be fun.'

'You forget. I'm your housekeeper. Your employee.'

'Maybe it's time we stopped all that nonsense. I've only contracted for you to stay until the end of the next week anyhow. Officially, this was your trial period. What do you say we stop pretending you're just an employee?'

'Cheapskate. You're just trying to get out of paying my wages. I don't think Lettie's going to be too thrilled,' she laughed. 'I'd love to see her face if we told her the truth. All the same, I'd prefer to remain as your housekeeper for these dinner parties. Then we'll give more thought to what happens next.'

'Do you want anything else?' Dom asked, putting down his napkin.

'Not sure,' she replied. He grinned and asked for a sweet menu.

'I'm not sure where you put all this food. How do you manage to stay slim?'

'I worry a lot,' she replied glibly.

The Truth Comes Out

While she prepared the Friday's vegetarian meal, Dom worked some more on the book collection. He came through from time to time to ask her advice. He sniffed appreciatively.

'I could become a full-time vegetarian if it smelt that good. What is there for me to taste?'

'Go away. You'll be eating it this evening. Who are the guests?'

'People from work. They sometimes stay overnight, but I didn't invite them this time.'

'You could have done.'

'I know. But it would have meant a lot of extra work for you and Jane, wouldn't it?'

'Yes, but it is your house. We are here to work for at least a while longer.'

'They'd probably have wanted to stay on for the weekend and that means loads more work and I didn't want it anyway.' He touched the back of her neck as he passed. She was trying to concentrate on stirring a sauce and practically dropped the wooden spoon.

'If you want a decent meal tonight, you'd better leave me to get on with it.'

'Do you want to join us tonight? For dinner I mean.'

'If you like.'

'I'd better warn you, they are computer buffs and will doubtless talk shop the entire evening.'

'In that case, I'll stick with a tray in the staff quarters. I can serve the food more easily, as it's evening and Jane will have gone home.'

He gave a huge, exaggerated sigh as he left her. She laughed and continued her chores.

* * *

The evening went well, though the couple hinted that they were slightly surprised not to have been invited to stay. Dom was careful to see that nobody drank more than they should, so they were able to drive home safely. As soon as they left, Dom came into the kitchen to find Lissa. Everything was neat and tidy and the dishwasher running. Of Lissa, there was no sign.

He went up the stairs, three at a time calling her name.

'In here,' she replied from her own room. She opened the door, ready for bed.

'Sorry. I felt too tired to stay up. I wasn't sure how long they were going to stay.'

'I'm obviously overworking you. Sorry but it's not for much longer.'

The next day, Lissa thought Dom seemed unusually restless and even slightly nervous. Every time she turned round, he seemed to be behind her, watching her. She had wondered if Dom would invite her to be his hostess again but he said nothing. With only one guest it was easy and she had not asked Jane to come in to serve on this occasion. Dom had readily agreed that it was unnecessary. She prepared the meal conscientiously, hoping to please him and his guest.

She opened the wine early, to allow it to breathe and arranged the table formally, setting both places at one end of the long table, to allow them to talk more easily. They would have drinks in the lounge first and Dom would call her when they were ready for the meal. He also insisted that he would answer the door himself, leaving her free to organise the cooking.

She gave it little thought, being somewhat more interested in what time the guest would leave. She rather hoped it wouldn't be too late for her own agenda to have a place. She was determined that she was going to tell him the truth about herself that evening.

When the doorbell rang, she peered out of the kitchen, hoping to get a glimpse of the visitor but Dom had already whisked him into the lounge.

She put the finishing touches to the meal and had the soup ready to heat as soon as it was required. She sat dreamily at the kitchen table, waiting for Dom's signal.

In the lounge, Dom had tried to relax into his role as host. He looked at Alistair Langham, this man who was the father of his beloved Lissa. He was tall and distinguished looking, his immaculate hair a dark silver-grey. He must be somewhere in his late fifties, Dom guessed and considerably younger than his own father had been. He could see where Lissa had inherited some of her genes.

'Didn't we meet when you were a boy?' asked Alistair. 'Seem to remember there was a youngster hanging round occasionally.'

'We may have done, sir.' It seemed important to maintain formality. 'I was away at school of course. Not here very often.'

'Remarkable collection of books your father had. I suppose that's why I am here? You have an interest in collecting? S'pose you can't have, if you're considering selling them. Great shame.'

'Well no, I don't. Not really. I'm more of a technology freak, in my own way. As a matter of fact, I'd actually forgotten you were a book collector yourself. That explains your remark about being offered first refusal. My mind was on other things at the time.'

He spoke slowly, realising the full implication of Lissa's knowledge. How could he have been so foolish not to have made this other connection? She must also have known the agent whose visit she had arranged.

'As I mentioned, I am certainly planning to dispose of some of the collection. The inheritance taxes are pretty horrendous these days.'

'In that case, I'd very much like to have a look at some of the books. I'd certainly like to get my hands on quite a number of Ted's rarities. He spent much more time on his collection than I ever have. Yes, there are several volumes I can remember. I'd be very interested in having a look at those. If you wouldn't mind, of course. I'd pay the proper value. Not asking for any favours. What do you say?'

'Certainly. I'm sure it's what my father would have wanted.'

'Let's get to it then. Why wait?' He put his drink down on the side table and rose to his feet.

'After dinner perhaps? Actually, sir, there is something else I'd rather like to discuss with you first. A very important, personal matter.'

'Go on. Though there's probably nothing more important to me than books, you realise.'

Dom smiled and hesitated. Everything had gone well so far but he was certain the next discussion, about Alistair's only daughter, was going to prove considerably more important than books.

'It's about Lissa.'

'My daughter? What's she got to do with anything?'

'Well sir, really, well . . . '

'Spit it out, boy.'

'I wondered if you'd give your permission for us to be married? I love her and I'd like to marry her.' The words tumbled out. It hadn't been at all the way he'd planned to break the news.

'Good God. Didn't even realise you knew her. Does she want to marry you?'

'I think so. I haven't actually asked her yet. I thought I should ask you first.'

'Very correct, I'm sure. How long has this been going on?'

'Well, not exactly for very . . . '

'You seem a nice enough young man. She could do worse. But it's entirely up to her. I'm quite beyond being able to control what my daughter wants to do. She seems to have taken it into her head that she's an adult. If you want to marry her, then I suppose she must be.' He looked angry when he spoke of his daughter and Dom felt slightly concerned.

'Well, thank you, sir,' Dom said, amazed by the apparent ease of the task he'd been dreading. Maybe his reputation wasn't as bad as he'd feared. 'I'll take it I have your approval? I'll ask her right away. Well, at the first possible opportunity. Perhaps you're ready to eat now? I'll go and tell my . . . er . . . cook.'

His heart pounding, he left the room. His grin was spreading uncontrolled. He went into the kitchen and took Lissa in his arms. He swung her round in his excitement and kissed her happily.

'What's all this about?' she laughed breathlessly.

'I'll tell you later. It's a surprise. We're ready for dinner now. I'm so happy, Lissa.' He whirled out of the kitchen in a most uncharacteristic manner. She shook her head. He was going mad, she thought but the thrill of having him so close was exhilarating enough.

Quickly she re-heated the soup and added cream, her own smile quite uncontrollable. Whoever the guest was, he certainly seemed to have brought some good news. Whatever was going on inside her, she needed to remain calm enough to serve the dinner in a competent, professional manner.

She loaded the plates on to a tray, smoothed her hair and went towards the dining room. She pushed open the door and practically dropped the tray. Dom swiftly moved towards her and took it from her.

'Daddy? What on earth . . . ?' She gazed at the two men. It was obvious that Dom knew exactly her relationship to Alistair.

'Lissa? What on earth are you doing?'

'Cooking your dinner, it seems. You knew.' She glared at Dom. How long had he known? This changed everything.

'My daughter? A servant? I don't think so. Damned insolent young pup. Using my daughter as some sort of servant. How dare you?'

He flung his napkin down on the

table, knocking over the elegant cut crystal wine glass as angrily he pushed his chair back. 'Bates told me some nonsense about you having a job. Is this it? How could you demean yourself this way?'

'You told me I was an empty headed waste of space. I think that was your exact phrase. I was determined to prove to you that I could hold down a job.'

'And how long have you been skivvying like this?'

'What do you mean, 'like this'? There's nothing wrong with the job I've been doing. Certainly not skivvying as you put it. You paid for me to learn to cook after all. I've been here a few weeks. Working. Properly working. And he didn't know who I was. At least, I didn't think he knew.' She paused to glare at him. 'But I've done a good job, haven't I, Dom?'

'I've certainly got no complaints,' Dom replied uneasily.

After his brief moment of euphoria, it

was all going dreadfully wrong. He had been an idiot to think his stupid, devious plan could work.

'I'm sure you haven't. Once you realised who she was, you must have been very well pleased. Get in with the family. Her money could certainly help you out of your inheritance tax crisis. Expecting me to write a cheque immediately, to settle your problem, were you?' His green eyes, exactly the same colour as his daughter's, Dom noticed, were flashing angrily.

'I promise you, I had no idea who she was, until one of my lunch guests saw her, the other day. I'd already realised the extent of my feelings well before I had any idea you were her father. It didn't take long for me to realise just how much I love her. She's a wonderful woman. Perfect in every way. I thought that if we talked, if you knew who I was, it might make a difference. My father would have been delighted if the daughter of his old friend became my wife.'

'You're a scheming, conniving, devious man. Your father would have been thoroughly ashamed of you. Employing my daughter as a . . . a cook. You're beneath contempt.'

'But I assure you, sir, I truly had no idea who she was when I employed her. She was a temp from an agency . . . and . . . '

'You can't expect me or her to believe that? You must have known who she was from the start.'

'No, sir. You're wrong. Truly. I employed her through an agency. If the truth be known, she isn't the greatest housekeeper in the world, but she can certainly cook like a dream. As a person, she is . . . well, she is the woman I'd hope to marry. If she'll have me of course.'

'I hope she shows some sense. After her last little escapade with a man, I sincerely hoped she'd learned her lesson. She's just a target for any get-rich-quick Johnny.'

'But, sir,' Dom protested.

'Do I have any say in this, at all?' shouted Lissa, unable to bear any more of this slanging match. 'Doesn't my opinion matter?'

'Of course it does, darling,' Dom said, realising he was still holding the tray of now congealing soup. He put it down and turned to Lissa, his arms held out to her.

'No. Get away from me. Doesn't anyone want to know what I think? No. Leave me alone. You'll confuse me if you touch me.'

'Touch her and I'll lay you flat,' Alistair yelled.

Dom was in no doubt that he would have done just that.

'Shut up, Daddy. It's time you realised that I'm not your little girl any more. I can make my own decisions.'

The man went scarlet with fury.

'In that case, I'll leave you to it. Don't you ever learn from your past mistakes? Men are only after you for one thing. My money. This one's no different. Stay here if you must. But don't expect to inherit a penny from me. I'll . . . I'll start a zoo . . . or found an old people's home, with your inheritance.'

'Fine. Go ahead. I can always get a job as a cook, any day. Dom will give me a reference, I'm sure.'

Alistair turned and stormed out of the room. They heard the front door slam and his car drove away from the house in an angry roar.

'Oh, Lissa, I'm so sorry. I've been a total idiot. Come here my darling. Let me hold you.'

'Keep away from me. Like I said. You'll confuse me if you touch me again. Did I actually hear you tell my father that you love me?'

'Yes.'

'Then why for heaven's sake didn't you tell me?'

'I hadn't realised just how much I love you until . . . well until now.'

'And didn't I hear you mention something about me being your wife? Marriage?'

'I wanted to ask your father's permission first. He has quite a reputation where his only daughter is concerned. Quite a justified reputation, I discover.'

'And exactly when did you decide that you wanted to marry me? Before or after you knew who I was?'

'Knowing who you were had nothing to do with it. I fell in love with you almost the first moment I met you, even if I didn't realise it at the time. You must have understood what we were beginning to mean to each other? I'd hinted at it and thought you realised what I was planning. I don't behave like this with just anyone, you know. I'm serious. I want to marry you. Please Lissa, say yes. You know it's what you want. What we both want.'

'I'm not sure about anything any more. You knew exactly who I was soon after we met and yet you said nothing. I so needed you to want me for myself, not just as my father's wealthy daughter. I can't bear to have this come between Daddy and me. He's always tried to do his best for me. Even if he does disinherit me to prove something. I can't, I won't marry you unless my father comes round. He means far too much to me.'

'I'd like your father's approval, of course I would. But with or without money, it's you I want. Your father's money means nothing. Truly.'

'But you admitted you're selling your father's books because you can't pay the taxes. How do I know you're not trying to con me? That it wasn't all a careful plan?'

'Oh, for heavens' sake. What is it with you and money? I don't care about money. I've got a large fortune of my own, anyway. Don't you realise that? The tax issue is something completely different. I don't want to sell this house and selling the books is a way of keeping it, without propping it up with my own company. I really don't have an interest in dusty old volumes. I'd like someone to have them who actually might appreciate them. I'd even make a gift of them to your father, if it would help.'

'I need time to think.'

'I need you.' He reached for her and despite her resistance, he drew her to him. She held herself rigid, trying to push him away.

'You mustn't. I won't do this. Dom, stop it now. You are still confusing me.'

He pressed his mouth against her own and she felt herself melting.

'Oh, my darling,' he gasped. 'Dearest, dearest Lissa. You do care for me, don't you? This is not quite the way I'd expected the evening to go.' He felt enormous relief that she hadn't pushed him away. Everything was going to be all right.

Suddenly, her expression hardened as she did finally push him away.

'I'm sorry. I shouldn't have done that,' she said. 'It was a big mistake. My last big mistake where you are concerned.'

'How can you say that? It was a kiss

that proved we do love each other.'

But she felt ashamed at her own weakness. Her father had been right all along. Men didn't want her. They wanted access to her fortune. She looked at the wrecked table and began to clear things away.

'Stop it,' Dom ordered. 'Stop it right there.'

'I'm paid to do a job, besides, there's food in the oven. It will be ruined. Probably burnt to a crisp.'

'I don't care about food. Ovens. Anything. I care about you, Lissa. Please say you'll marry me.'

'I can't, Dom. Not now. You should have told me that you knew who I was. If only you'd told me that you loved me, before you knew who I was. I wonder, would you still have wanted me? This changes everything.'

'Your father certainly did a job on you, didn't he? He doesn't want anyone else to have his precious little Daddy's Girl. What does he expect of you? That you'll stay with him all your life? Stay with him as long as he lives? What happens when he's no longer around? Who'll make your decisions then? Grow up, Lissa. Take happiness when it's offered or you'll end up as empty and selfish as he is. Maybe you're right. You should leave now.'

She turned and left the room. She went up to her room and stuffed some of her clothes into her bag. She didn't bother to clear the drawers or the bathroom. She wanted to get right away as quickly as possible. Escape from this scene. The whole of this place held too many memories. Too many reminders of her very short spell of happiness. She should have known better. She should have taken her father's advice more seriously.

Realisation Dawns On Lissa

There was a light burning in her father's study when Lissa arrived back home. She parked her hired car beside her father's car and pushed at the door. It was locked. She didn't even have a key. She hammered at the door. After several minutes, Bates came to open it.

'Miss Lissa? What on earth are you doing back here at this time of night?'

'Is it late? Sorry, I hadn't realised.'

'No, no. Come in. Can I get you something? Hot chocolate maybe?' She smiled. Whenever she'd had a problem as a child, Bates had produced a cup of hot chocolate. She didn't even like it very much, but it was a kind thought and comfortingly familiar.

'No thanks. I think I may need a

brandy tonight. I'll go and see my father.'

'I'm not sure it would be a good idea. I think he's . . . well, he's had a bit of an upset over something. He wouldn't say what it was. Went out for dinner and came back early. He wouldn't have any food, even though Mrs Bates offered him all sorts. So you see, he's in a terrible mood and I don't want you to be upset as well.' Bates's kindly face looked troubled. He had always tried to warn her if her father was ill-humoured.

'I know all about it. It's about me. I need to sort out a few things with him. Thanks for your concern though, but don't worry, dear Bates. I'm a big girl now.'

'Right you are, Miss. I'll leave you to it. Ring the bell if you want anything. Anything at all.'

'You do look after me well, you and Mrs Bates. Thank you. Not just for now, but for all the kindnesses over the years.' He gave a little half bow and walked away slowly.

He's getting to be an old man, she realised with a start. It seemed he'd always been part of her life. She turned to tap on the study door and pushed it open.

'So. Come to your senses, have you?' Alistair said gruffly.

'That was quite a scene. I was ashamed of you.'

'I was only looking out for you. Insolent young pup. His own father would probably have disinherited him if he'd known how he'd behaved. Fancy trying to worm his way into our family like that. Not that you are entirely without blame. How could you stoop so low? Demeaning yourself.'

'Really, you're such a snob, Daddy. I suppose it isn't demeaning for a poor old man like Bates to run round looking after us?'

'That's an entirely different matter. It's his job. And don't let him hear you calling him old. Plenty of life left in him yet.'

'Be nice if he could have the time to

enjoy it, then. As for Dom, well, everything was going fantastically well, until he discovered I was your daughter. I'm beginning to think it's a curse. At least I know you won't be able to pay him off. He's got plenty of his own money. I don't know yet what I'm going to do long term. I need some time to think. I'm going to bed now. Assuming, of course that you don't intend to ban me from my own home?'

'Don't be silly, darling. You're always uppermost in my thoughts. That's why I'm always trying to do my best for you, however much you may resent it.'

'Really?' she said scornfully. 'I'll see you in the morning.'

★ ★ ★

She was getting accustomed to sleepless nights. Tears filled her eyes when she thought about their all too brief spell of thinking that she and Dom really cared about each other. She wasn't fully convinced it was quite over yet but all the same, her father's suggestion could not be dismissed. Perhaps her own lack of experience had allowed her to be duped.

Maybe Dom's fortune wasn't quite as large as he'd suggested. It would probably be a good ploy to pretend one didn't care at all about money or status, especially if someone who was obviously very rich came into his life. She tried to tell herself that he couldn't possibly have known that she would turn up as his housekeeper. He'd applied for someone to work for him, well before she'd arrived at the agency. Perhaps it was merely fortuitous, after all.

Or maybe he'd recognised her and known exactly who she was from the moment she arrived. She had been aware of that photograph in the magazine and most probably he'd seen it too. Once he'd recognised her, he'd set about worming his way into her affections right from the start.

She felt ashamed and foolish. No

wonder her father had always seen the necessity to protect her. She obviously needed it. In the darkness of her own room, she blushed fiery red. She doubted she would ever be able to forgive Dom for what she was going through now.

★　★　★

She came down late the next morning. Her father was still sitting at the breakfast table, reading his paper.

'There's coffee on the side,' he murmured. 'Or ring Bates and ask for fresh if it's too stewed.'

'It's OK. This will do. I'll have some juice anyhow.'

'How are you feeling this morning?' he asked.

'Ghastly. I didn't sleep.'

'He's probably been working you too hard over the past weeks. Getting his money's worth no doubt. You're not used to it. Have a quiet day. Relax a bit.'

'I've things to do,' she said coldly. 'I have to go into town and formally resign from my job, for one thing. I don't suppose the agency will be too pleased. The woman did me a favour taking me on when I've so few qualifications for anything.'

'Obviously, I don't understand you one little bit. But it saddens me. I'm so sorry if I have upset you. I never wanted to upset you. You are all I have in this world, to really care about. Please, let's be friends again. And whatever you think, I truly want you to be happy. With the right man.'

'But does he really exist? Will any man ever be allowed to be the right man?'

'Of course. One day there will be that indefinable spark. You'll know. You'll be ready to give everything to him.'

'I thought I'd found that with Dom,' she whispered sadly.

'At least you should feel relieved I sorted this out. You'd hate yourself.'

'Of course,' she croaked.

'Look, I've got an idea,' he said. 'I have to visit the Far East. I'm leaving next week. Singapore. Hong Kong. Why not come too and we'll have a bit of a holiday when I've finished my business. Take a look at Malaysia. Indonesia. Anywhere you like. What do you say?

'You can have a few days in London first. Do some shopping. Buy yourself a few nice things for the trip. We'll have some fun. Like we used to. It's ages since we had one of our little jaunts.'

'I don't know, Daddy. Thanks anyway.'

'Say you'll give it some thought, at least. I'd like it. There are so many things we need to talk about.'

'OK. I'll think about it.'

Lissa decided she couldn't face an actual visit to Lettie Jenkins and decided to telephone. The wretched woman sounded almost triumphant.

'I'll get on to Mr Wetherill right away,' she crowed. 'Explain that I took you on out of pity and give him my most profound apologies. Perhaps he will take back Elsie Smythe. An excellent lady. Wonderful credentials.'

'Whatever,' Lissa said wearily.

'You'd better let me have an address where you'll be staying. I'll send on your wages. You did manage to work for a few weeks after all. I expect you'll be grateful for something to tide you over. What's your address?'

'Ingleton Manor,' she began.

'Not The Ingleton Manor? Surely Mr Langham hasn't given you a job? I've sent him a lot of people. Waitresses and such. He didn't say anything to me about needing new staff. I didn't realise he was looking for a housekeeper.'

'He wasn't. Isn't. He's my father as a matter of fact.'

'Miss Langham. Of course. Now, why didn't I recognise that you are your father's daughter?' The woman's tone had completely changed. She was becoming sickeningly obsequious.

'Why should you? I didn't want you to know anything. Now, if there's nothing more. Send me anything you need me to sign by post. Goodbye.'

She plopped the phone down, smiling to herself. She'd almost have enjoyed seeing Lettie's face when she realised the truth.

She mooched about listlessly. She went out to the stables and took her mare for a short ride. Nothing seemed to hold its usual pleasure and she snapped inexcusably at the boy who came in to see to the horses.

She went round to the swimming pool and dipped her foot in to see how warm it was. She shed her clothes and dived in. There was no-one she cared about.

She swam several punishingly fast lengths, as if the movement would somehow expunge the feeling of guilt and self-loathing that she was feeling. Panting, she climbed out and showered before finding a robe.

She padded through the hall, leaving damp footprints on the polished parquet floor. There was a message on the telephone pad. Dominic Wetherill phoned. Would she please call back as soon as she got this message? Would she heck. If he thought he could get round her . . .

'Oh there you are, Miss Lissa. Domin . . . '

'Yes I saw the message. Thanks, Bates. Look, I'm sorry. I've made wet prints all over the floor. I didn't think.' Bates stared in amazement. She had always left dirty marks of one sort or another.

'Don't worry, Miss. They'll soon come off.'

She went to her room and looked for her trousers. They'd been worn a couple of times at Dom's house, but she'd thought they'd do again. She couldn't find them. In fact, everything she'd brought back had disappeared. Mrs Bates must have taken everything to be laundered.

Lissa felt guilty. She had always taken for granted that her clothes were hung up for her, that they were clean and pressed whenever she wanted them. She realised that she had always been rather a spoilt brat. Twenty-three and she was still being looked after like a baby. She heard the phone ring again and Bates answering it. He came to her door and knocked.

'Mr Wetherill on the telephone, Miss. Are you at home?'

She shook her head. 'I don't want to speak to him just yet.'

'I'll say I was unable to find you.'

'Thanks, Bates. You're very good to me.'

★   ★   ★

When her father returned that evening, she had almost made up her mind to go away with him. At least it would give her time to get over Dom. If she found she couldn't manage without him, she could return and see what might be salvaged of the situation . . . if anything.

There was a typed envelope waiting on the hall table the next morning. She slit it open. There was a rather angry letter from Lettie Jenkins, complaining about her lack of consideration, her lack of discipline and the fact that the agency had recently been deprived of a client. All traces of her obsequious words had gone.

Evidently, Dom had not taken Elsie back, nor anyone else from the agency. Lissa gave a sardonic smile. Even if she was the daughter of a very wealthy man, it was not enough to appease Lettie.

She looked into the envelope again. There was a cheque. It covered her wages for the time she had spent at Templars, with a few deductions that were evidently normal. The final total left her open-mouthed. It would scarcely have bought her a decent pair of shoes. She'd even spent nearly that much on a T-shirt with the right label. Was that amount really all that people earned? How on earth did they manage?

She must ask her father what Mr and Mrs Bates were paid. She hoped it was considerably more than this. She sat thinking for a while. She knew nothing about anything when it came to it.

When Dom had talked of inheritance taxes, what sort of sum could he be talking about? She was completely unaware of the real cost of anything. She always paid for things by credit card and the bills were sent to her father. Did any of it matter?

She was probably already too old to change very much. All the same, she decided that she wouldn't bother to buy more things for the trip. She could easily make do with what she already had. She flung the cheque down on to her dressing-table.

★　★　★

A week later, Lissa and Alistair were flying into a rather damp Singapore. It was dark as they arrived and they watched the lights reflecting on the wet tarmac.

As they emerged from the airport, the humid air hit them like a sauna.

'I always forget this first moment, when you realise it isn't just the air-conditioning gone wrong. This is what it's like all the time. I suppose people must get used to it eventually.'

'They are used to air-conditioning like the rest of us. Now, we should have a car waiting somewhere. Over there, darling.' Alistair relished having people at his beck and call, all over the world. He liked to be recognised and welcomed and always used the same drivers and hotels when he visited places.

They were driven along the road from the airport, where the rows of restaurants, huge tenement buildings and crowded streets flashed by their luxurious car. Brash lights reflected on the water as they passed a row of popular restaurants.

At last, they arrived at their hotel. It was built alongside the Singapore River, a glorious mixture of traditional architecture and modern comfort. The staff were welcoming and did all they could to ensure their important visitors had everything they could possibly need.

Lissa watched her father lapping up the attention and felt slightly sickened. She had begun to know exactly how much effort went into the seemingly easy welcome and provision of their needs.

'I'm going to have an early night,' Lissa told him. 'I'll have a bath and settle down. I'm absolutely shattered.'

'But what about dinner?' Alistair protested. 'I can't be expected to eat alone.'

'I'm sorry, but I really can't eat a large meal. I'll get a sandwich sent up. I'll see you in the morning.'

She couldn't wait to be alone and be able to spend time thinking of Dom. She was missing him more and more and was already bitterly regretting her impulsive actions. Now she was so far away from home, she desperately wanted to be near him.

How could anyone she had only known for so short a time, have become so important to her? She thought of his blue, blue eyes. His more serious expression when he was trying to show her the computer games he designed. Such imagination. Such enthusiasm.

She felt tears spring to her eyes. Had she spoiled everything? Had she allowed her father to spoil everything? She hoped not. She believed that he truly cared for her. He must still want to talk to her, judging by the number of calls he'd made. He'd been phoning several times every day, right up to their departure. But she'd needed time to think and get her mind back into some sort of order.

Before she and her father had left, she had instructed Bates to say she was away indefinitely. She glanced at her watch, wondering whether it was too late to call Bates and find out if he really had passed on the message. It would be too early in the morning. Though Bates would never object, she knew it was unfair to wake him.

'Oh, Dom, what have I done.' she moaned into her pillow.

While her father conducted his business in the city, she spent the days shopping and joining several of the tourist strips that everyone was so keen to promote. She bought a few things but her heart was not really in the Singapore shopping experience she had once loved so much. She stared at stalls full of tourist souvenirs.

She looked at several small pewter creatures, a speciality of the area, knowing that if Dom had been here, he would almost certainly have bought at least one for her.

She walked away, feeling sad and lonely. Her father encouraged her to buy things but she felt constantly troubled by the poverty she could see beneath the surface. This was a relatively wealthy place but there was still a desperate need for many of the residents. She knew they probably didn't even earn anything like as much as her own meagre salary as housekeeper, had been.

Her father was being most solicitous, obviously trying very hard to make up for what she'd mistaken as his desire to control her. The real truth was that he was scared of someone hurting his precious daughter. He'd been hurt himself on too many occasions and learned his own difficult lessons. He desperately wanted to protect her from everything unpleasant.

It was not easy to know where the limitations should be. He also admitted if only to himself, that he dreaded the thought of her living a life separate from his own. But he was being too selfish. Guiltily he realised that one day soon, he would also have to take her into his confidence about his own private life.

Lissa wandered through her third huge shopping mall of the morning. She stopped suddenly, transfixed by someone. She watched the man walking in front of her. Tall. Jet black hair, curling slightly round his collar. It had to be some sort of miracle, but there was Dom, walking just a few paces ahead of her. She ran forward, touching his arm to stop him.

'Dom. What on earth are you doi . . . ' her voice trailed away as the man turned round, puzzled. 'Oh, I'm so sorry. I mistook you for someone I know.' Embarrassed, she walked away. It showed how much the man was on her mind. He didn't really look like Dom at all.

She stopped again, staring unseeingly into a shop window. She could barely remember what Dom looked like. She felt scared at yet another loss. It was altogether too scary, the way the mind played tricks.

When the Singapore stage of their trip was over, they moved on to Hong Kong. The heat seemed more oppressive than ever. Alistair tried to spend a little more time with her, worried by her pale face and lack of energy.

'You could always call Dominic, you know, if that's what is troubling you. He isn't the worst of your choices, I suppose. Why don't you try to find out what he's doing?' he said in desperation over dinner, one evening. He hated even to think he might have made a mistake, but he couldn't bear to see Lissa so despondent.

'How can I? I refused to speak to him when he called me at home. No, I just have to get over him. It'll be fine. What are your plans for tomorrow?' she asked as brightly as she could.

'I thought we might hire a cruise boat. There are a few people I'd like to entertain. We could motor along through the harbour and out among the islands. What do you say?'

'Sounds nice. Anyone I know?'

'Probably a few familiar faces among them. I'll set it up then. Late afternoon, so we catch the sunset. Get yourself something nice to wear.'

'Sounds lovely,' she tried to enthuse. She spent the afternoon swimming in the hotel pool, visiting the spa and finally having her hair done. She went into the hotel boutique and bought a new silk dress in a vibrant shade of emerald green. She knew it would please her father to see her dressing up for his party and she hoped it might also lift her from the depression she had been feeling since their arrival.

At five o'clock, the reception desk called her to say her car was waiting. There was a long escalator leading down into the foyer, shiny glass mirrors everywhere sent lights flashing everywhere and marble floors shone with a polish that must have taken hours of work each day.

She smiled at a young girl dressed in the beige tunic and trousers of the hotel cleaning staff. The girl looked down and bowed her head. Lissa wanted to go and speak to her but knew it might cause embarrassment.

Staff were supposed to be unobtrusive at all times and the fact she had been noticed might cause the girl to be scolded by her bosses. Before her time spent as a so-called housekeeper, she would not even have noticed anyone working. With a small sigh, she went out to the large limousine her father had organised. The chauffeur bowed as he closed the door behind her. The engine had been left running to ensure that the air-conditioning met with her approval.

'There's a small fridge in the back,' he told her. 'Cold drink for you, if you wish.'

'Thanks, but I'm fine. It isn't far to the harbour, is it?'

'We have a little drive. Mr Langham has chosen a small pier for his journey as it's more peaceful.'

She sat back in the well upholstered seats, watching the evening multitudes milling through crowded streets. The evening food vendors were taking up kerb-side pitches, each with two large woks balanced on a yoke and small paraffin stoves set up on the pavement ready to begin cooking.

British law would never allow such hazards to be part of city life. She gave a sigh, wondering why her father had organised a car just for her. Where was he? After almost half an hour, they drew up at a quiet pier where a large boat was moored.

Several male servants in immaculate white suits, stood by the gangplank, ready to assist guests aboard and ready with trays of champagne to hand out once they were on board. Lissa accepted a glass when she stepped on to the deck. It was wet with condensation in the warm evening. She drank it down quickly so that it didn't get any warmer.

She thanked the waiter and went in search of her father.

He was standing in the air-conditioned cabin, surrounded by expensively-dressed women and men in light coloured evening suits. She was glad she had dressed up in this elegant company. All the same, she was conscious of the extravagant, conspicuous spending of the whole scene. Alistair crossed to her and put his arm round her shoulders.

'Darling. You look stunning. Thank

you for taking such trouble and for coming, of course. You may know a few of the folks here. Probably not seen them for years but they'll be delighted with you.' A large woman, perspiring heavily despite the chill of the air-conditioning, came towards them.

'Don't tell me this is your little one. She's so grown up. I thought she was still a schoolgirl but the years do fly by.'

'This is Constance. Constance Jerome. You met her when you were small. Her husband works in the Northern branch.'

'Hello. Yes, of course I remember you. I think I was only small when we last met so it must be some years ago. Are you here on business?'

'Oh, yes. I doubt many of us come here for the climate. Always enjoy a bit of shopping and pick up a few bargains, of course. Wonderful prices for many things here.'

'Indeed. But a lot of poverty, too.'

Lissa mingled with her father's guests, politely chatting to them all and wishing she could be somewhere cooler.

They all went out on the deck to look at the sunset, a spectacular rosy blush to the sky with the islands in the bay showing sharp contrast as the light quickly failed.

'Lovely, isn't it, darling?' her father said, standing close to her. 'Glad to see you're over all that nonsense with that man,' Alistair whispered to her during the evening. 'I don't want my girl settling for some jumped up nobody. I'll find you the right man one day. I promise.' He sounded as though it was a matter of selecting someone from the supermarket shelves. 'Some more champagne?'

'No thanks, Daddy. I'm suffering a bit from the heat. It feels as if someone needs to open some windows even in the open air. I rather long for the fresh air of the English summer. I think I might have to desert you soon. It's been a lovely trip, but I feel quite drained.'

'You do look a little pale. Are you feeling all right?'

'Not sure. I guess it's just the heat.

Once we dock, I'll take my leave of you all.'

'As you like. Thank you again for coming. You've been charming everyone. You're a great hit.'

★   ★   ★

When they arrived back at the pier, she made her excuses and was one of the first to leave. There was talk of going on somewhere but she needed to lie down and was driven back to the hotel. She felt distinctly unwell. It must have been the heat or some wretched bug she must have caught. She felt queasy and slightly dizzy. There was always this unrelenting heat whenever they were outside the air-conditioning of the hotel.

The next morning, Lissa felt worse than ever. Her father wanted to call the hotel doctor but she refused.

'I'll be fine. If I take it easy today, I should be better soon. It must be something I've eaten that doesn't agree.

Or maybe I've got heat stroke. Or even a bug.'

'All the same, I'd like you to get checked out with a doctor.'

'I promise. If I don't feel better later, I'll call the hotel doctor. Now, go off and do your work.'

All the rest of the day she felt ill. She was actually sick and lay down on her bed. She fell asleep and when her father finally phoned to ask her to join him for lunch, she felt too bad even to contemplate eating.

'Call the doctor immediately. You must have food poisoning. I can't disappoint my guests but I won't stay long. Please, call the doctor. Or shall I do it?'

'No, I'll call. Promise.' She dropped the phone and laid back. She remembered nothing more until her father returned later. He asked at the reception if she had seen the doctor and when they said nothing had been seen of Lissa, he demanded that the manager open her room. She came round as she was being whisked off to hospital.

The next few days passed in a blur. She had contracted a severe bout of food poisoning and had become dehydrated and was a very sick girl. Her father sat beside her bed for hours, clad in a surgical mask. He even found a long forgotten prayer somewhere in his mind and prayed for his daughter's return to health. It was many hours before she was even capable of speech.

'Daddy? I'm sorry.' Her voice wavered and it took her some time to speak the words.

'It's all right, darling. Quiet now. I'm just glad you're making some sort of recovery. You've been very ill.'

'What time is it?' she asked, confused by his words.

'Don't worry about it. You've been asleep for two whole days. We've been very worried about you.'

'What do you mean . . . two days? What day is it?'

'It doesn't matter. You've been right

out of it. They say you're on the mend now.'

She closed her eyes again and reflected on his words. Through her fuzzy brain, she began to remember things that had been happening. Dom. Where was Dom? Why wasn't he here? She loved him, didn't she? And he loved her. They were getting married, weren't they?

'Dom? Where's Dom? Was he here?'

'Now then, my dear. Just try to relax. Get some sleep.'

* * *

A few days later, she was feeling better.

'Daddy, I'm sorry but I really want to go home. I need to get back to a cooler climate and some sort of normality. I hate the poverty everywhere. It's not just here. I'm actually feeling bad about being so rich. Guilty that I can spend money like water. Not ever thinking twice about buying clothes or anything else.'

'Don't forget we're actually helping the local community by buying their goods and services.'

'Maybe you're right, but I can't take it any more. I've learned so many lessons since I began my working life.'

Alistair frowned. He hated the fact that she had found it necessary to work and regretted his harsh words to her all those weeks ago.

'I'm sorry about my outburst. I was unfair and never meant you to take it so seriously. I've been under a certain amount of strain lately. There are things we need to talk about. Personal things I've been neglecting for much too long.'

'When we're home again, Daddy. But now, I feel I have to return to England.'

'But there is something I need to say. Something I have to tell you.' He saw her expression of frustration followed by one of deepest unhappiness. 'You're still hankering after that man, aren't you?'

She nodded, her cheeks colouring slightly. Her heart was racing at the very thought of seeing Dom again.

'Then you should go. Follow your heart but, please, don't give it away lightly. You're much too precious to me.'

'Trust me, Daddy. I'm a big girl now.'

'So you say. Now, I have a couple of days of meetings, so I hope you'll occupy yourself until I'm ready to go.'

She booked a flight and left without even saying goodbye. She knew her father would be so busy that it could be a day or two before he realised that she had left for England.

A Confrontation Occurs

After Lissa's rapid departure from his home, Dom felt as if he had received a body blow right in the gut. He simply couldn't believe any of it. How could she have doubted that he was sincere in his feelings towards her? He'd tried to do everything for the best. Clearly, he'd quite underestimated the hold Alistair Langham had over his daughter.

He punched his fist into the other palm, cursing his own stupidity at not asking her first. Every time he'd tried to call her, he was fobbed off by that wretched Bates. At first he'd doubted his messages were being passed on but finally, he was satisfied that Lissa was refusing to speak to him.

The nights were the worst. The sheer gut-wrenching ache, that left him almost shaking, frightened him through and through. Nobody had ever had that effect on him before. He hardly slept. Work was piling up.

When the book dealer telephoned to arrange to collect the books for the sale, he snapped at the innocent man and told him he'd changed his mind. He slammed the phone down, not bothering to explain.

Finally, he left the house and went to London for a few days. But nothing was any better there. The next time he called Lissa's home, Bates told him she and her father had gone away for an extended holiday. He managed to discover they had gone to the Far East but could glean no more details, apart from a brief mention of Singapore.

After another few days, he'd had enough. He booked a ticket to Singapore and began his search. He tried to think of the sort of places Alistair might have stayed. There were so many hundreds of hotels in the city, it seemed a fruitless search.

He tried the most expensive modern hotels; the traditional Raffles and other similar places, but to no avail. He wondered if they had an apartment in the city and began to check telephone numbers but it was all fruitless.

After a couple of very depressing days, he finally discovered, with the help of his own brand of charm and several dollar bills, that the couple he sought had checked out two days earlier, bound for Hong Kong. He even managed to obtain a forwarding address.

In higher spirits than he'd known for several days, he booked a flight to Hong Kong for the next day. He managed to get a decent night's sleep for once, happy in the knowledge that he would be catching up with Lissa the following day. He must make her realise that he couldn't live without her. If her father chose to disinherit her, so be it. He had more than enough money for the most extravagant needs anyone could possibly have.

The oppressive heat of Hong Kong didn't trouble Dom. His mind was totally focussed on his quest. He took a taxi from the airport, straight to the hotel where he believed the pair were staying. At the reception, he asked for Alistair and Lissa's room numbers, but they refused to tell him.

'I'm sorry, sir. Confidentiality. Our guests deserve to have their privacy. You must understand.'

'For heaven's sake. I only want to ask the lady to marry me.' He was shouting and attracting the attention of several other guests who were standing in the cool marbled area. It was the most interesting event of their day, so far.

'Please sir, don't shout, sir. I do sympathise. If you'd like to leave a message, I will contact Mr Langham. That is the best I can offer.' The implacable gaze of the woman receptionist was infuriating.

'It is not Mr Langham I want to see. It is his daughter, Miss Langham,' he growled.

'Actually, I'm afraid Miss Langham checked out this morning.'

'What? She can't have done. I've just flown in from Singapore especially to see her.' He was almost shouting again.

'Please sir. I shall have to ask you to leave if you don't keep your voice down. You are disturbing our other guests.'

'Where has she gone?' The receptionist shook her head again. 'Then I must talk to Mr Langham. Please phone his room and ask him to speak to me. Tell him it's Dominic Wetherill.'

Impatiently, he stood drumming his fingers on the luxurious marble surface. Several people were standing nearby, obviously waiting to see what happened next. The receptionist put the phone down.

'I'm sorry, sir. There is no answer from his suite.'

'Can you have him paged then? It's most important that I speak with him urgently.'

After several minutes longer and considerable persuasion on his part, a messenger was sent to the numerous restaurants and other facilities. A discreet message board with Alistair's name on it, was taken into each room in turn. After what seemed like an eternity, the messenger returned.

If Alistair was anywhere in the hotel, he was not responding. In desperation, Dom booked a room. If he had to stand by the main door for the entire night, he would do it. At least having a room here meant that he had a right to stay in the place.

It was almost midnight when Alistair finally returned. Dom leapt to his feet and stopped him at the reception desk.

'Mr Langham. Dom Wetherill. You remember me?'

'You? What on earth are you doing here?'

'Waiting for you. I came to find Lissa but they tell me she's left. Whatever you think of me sir, I have to ask her to marry me just once more. I am desperate. I really do want to marry her. Whatever you say or do, it's up to her. Until I hear it from her own mouth. I won't believe that she doesn't want me.'

To his amazement, Alistair burst out laughing.

'I'll give you one thing. You're at least persistent. Tracked us right out here, did you? Shows a bit of guts, I suppose. But too bad. It's done you no good. She's gone. She left without saying goodbye. Don't know where she is now.' His face looked smug. Dom thought, resisting the temptation to throw a punch at this irritating man.

'Is there still a chance that you won't object to my marrying your daughter?' Dom asked cautiously. Alistair's earlier amusement had given him the slightest hope. 'I've never known anyone like her. I love her with all my heart.'

Alistair snorted. He started at Dom and gave a slight sneer.

'She's got over you. She's already forgotten you, I'm afraid. She left in such a hurry, I suspect she's met up with someone and taken off with him.'

'Really,' Dom said, knowing the man

was lying. He would never have allowed his precious daughter to go off with a near stranger. 'And where did she . . . or they go?'

'I don't know! Now, get out of my way. I don't know where she is. Do you understand me?' His anger and exasperation were now quite evident. 'I don't know where she is or what she's doing.' His distress did seem genuine. 'Now, clear off out of my sight. You're the cause of all this trouble. If I ever see you again, I'll get the law to sort you out. Understand me? and if I ever learn you've laid one finger on my daughter, I'll . . . I'll . . . '

'It's all right, sir. Your message is quite clear.' He turned away and went up to his room. In a strange way, he could understand the anxiety of the man. He also felt a high degree of anxiety, wondering where Lissa had gone.

He lay on the bed, actually beginning to feel quite chilled by the intensity of the air-conditioning. What should he do next? It seemed a waste not to see something of this vibrant city. There were a few business calls he could make. He'd stay on for a few days and see what happened.

What lousy timing, he cursed. He'd missed her by only a few hours. If he'd got here sooner, they could have spent time together, discovering the city, and probably having such a good time. He didn't believe for a moment that she had indeed gone away with another man. That was merely Alistair's bluster to cover his own concern.

Dom managed to arrange a couple of business appointments for the following day. He dealt with a number of companies in the Far East and hoped that at least he could save something from his abortive trip.

After two days, he had taken as much as he could stand. He knew he must accept that he had lost Lissa. That it was too late. Just when he had finally realised that she was the love of his life he had lost her. Now he needed to return to his father's home, sort things out and move back to London. Then he would be free to resume his proper life.

His creative world of computer games must eventually be able to interest and absorb him again. He kept repeating to himself that he must accept that he had lost her. He had lost Lissa forever. If she wanted to see him, she would have called or at least tried to contact him. Damn and blast, he muttered.

Dominic Wetherill finally reached his old family home some time near midnight, a couple of days later. He tumbled into his bed, weary and despondent. He'd flown halfway round the world to find the woman he loved, only to discover that she had disappeared. Maybe he could contact the kindly old man, Bates wasn't it? Perhaps he would help provide him with some clues. He wondered what time the man went up to bed but decided that he should at least wait until the following morning. He fell into an exhausted sleep.

When he awoke, heavy and unrested, he heard someone moving around downstairs. In his jet-lagged, dreamlike state, he wondered if Lissa had come back and was at this moment, making breakfast for them both. The power of wishful thinking, he mused. As he came to, he realised Jane must have arrived for her morning's work and he hurried down. The girl was in the kitchen, brewing coffee for herself and Mrs Rowley. She gave a guilty start as Dom came into the kitchen.

'Oh, I'm sorry, sir,' she saw his slight frown at the use of the word. 'Mr Dom, I mean. I didn't know you were back. You should have let us know and I could have got things ready for you. Good trip?' she asked.

'Not really. I could murder some of that coffee. Think I must be jet-lagged or something.'

'You don't look too good,' Jane told him. In truth, he looked dreadful, she thought. Pale, heavy eyed and with almost two days' beard growth. 'Is there anything wrong?'

'Not really. I suppose Lissa hasn't phoned?' He took the mug of coffee she held out and took a long swig.

'Lissa? No Si . . . Mr Dom. I've kept a list of all your messages. There was one caller who didn't leave a message. I got there too late to catch the phone. I did that number recall thing and I wrote the number down in case you recognised it. Not one I know. That agency woman phoned again to see if you wanted a new housekeeper. Elsie wants to come back, apparently.'

'I doubt I'll be staying here for very long. I'm planning to go back to London. I might sell this place. It's too big for one person.'

'Oh, you can't. You can't get rid of this place. It's your family home. Your poor father would turn over in his grave.' Jane bit her lip. She was being much too familiar.

'Maybe. But you must admit it's hardly economical to keep it for one person who is only planning to be here for only a few weeks a year.'

'Maybe you'll settle one day. Have a family.'

'Some chance. I'm not mad keen on kids anyhow. Except as potential customers for my games, of course. No, I suspect I'm going to stay a bachelor for ever now.'

Jane gulped. How could such a drop dead gorgeous man ever think that? She knew that Lissa had been pretty smitten. Maybe she'd come back at some stage. She and Mrs Rowley had been wildly speculating, ever since Dom's mad dash overseas. Something must have happened, they both knew. For one thing, there was the way he'd been moping around since Lissa's sudden departure.

'Give me the list of phone calls. I'd better get things moving.' Jane went into the study and came back with a pad of neatly written names and numbers. 'Thanks, Jane. That's splendid. You did a really good job.'

The girl blushed and smiled, pleased with the praise. He quickly scanned the list. Nothing too important. He glanced at the unknown caller she had mentioned. Good for her, he thought. Showed initiative, finding out the number. It wasn't one he recognised. Probably a mobile, he thought. He went into the study and dialled. A standard mobile answering service.

'Someone from this number called me. Dominic Wetherill. Please call again if it's important.'

He sorted through his mail and tried to find some sort of occupation that might absorb him again and take his mind off his worries. The phone rang several times and he pounced on it each time, sending up small prayers that it might be Lissa. It was just as bad as the days before he went away. Nothing had changed. He could concentrate on nothing. Whatever he looked at seemed to remind him of Lissa and he felt dejected.

The phone rang again.

'Dom?'

It was her. Lissa. His heart began pounding at the sound of her voice.

'Lissa? Is that really you? I've been frantic. Where are you?'

'Hello, Dom. Yes, it's me.' Already she was feeling weak at the knees, just hearing his voice again. 'I'm at home.' However weak she felt though, she must be cautious.

'Lissa, Lissa,' he kept repeating. 'Do you realise I've been chasing you half way round the world? I was in Hong Kong yesterday. Hoping to meet up with you.'

'But I left the day before. Why on earth did you go there?' Her heart was now pounding totally out of control. He must really have cared to go to such lengths.

'I simply had to find you. I don't seem to be able to live without you. I was nearly going frantic when you went away. Please come over.'

'I'm not sure I should,' she said doubtfully.

'Why not?'

'It might be dangerous.'

'What rubbish. Lissa, we must talk. Please say you'll come over.'

'I'll think about it, Dom.'

'But you seemed so certain that you had some feelings for me at one time. What did I do that was so very wrong? You surely know how I feel about you.'

'Do I?' she said softly. 'You knew who I was. Who my father is. How do I really know it's me you say you care for? How do I know that it isn't just my father's money?' She was fighting the demon that said of course he was genuine and the one her father believed, telling her that Dom was after her fortune.

Suddenly, he hung up on her. She stared at the phone. She put it down, feeling desperately hurt. He had left a message on her mobile, hadn't he? He had sounded as if he genuinely wanted to speak to her. Perhaps he expected her to change her mind knowing that he'd follow her to Hong Kong. Her own doubts must have pushed him too far. He was only prepared to allow her so much, obviously.

Fifteen minutes later, there was hammering on the door. The bell rang in long, unbroken peals. Bates hurried out from the kitchen but Lissa beat him to it. She pulled the heavy door open and there was Dom. He was still unshaven and his clothes looked as if they had been slept in, as indeed they had.

'Dom. I wasn't expecting you. I thought you'd hung up on me.'

'Only because I had to see you. I heard your voice again and that was enough to convince me.'

'You didn't even know I was here. Or where I lived.'

'Of course I knew. For some time, I was camping in the lane outside, when I thought you might only be pretending to have gone away. That was way before I decided to follow you to the Far East. I wanted to know the truth or if it was your guard dog, simply trying to get rid of me.'

'You'd better come in,' she said at last, holding the door open for him.

'Is everything all right, Miss?' Bates asked, cautiously standing in the rather grand hall. 'I can call for someone if not.'

'It's fine, Bates. Thank you. This is Dominic Wetherill. Son of my father's old friend, Ted Wetherill.'

'Right you are, Miss. Will you be wanting coffee?'

Dom nodded gratefully.

'Thanks, Bates. And some of Mrs Bates's special biscuits, please, if there are any. You'd better come into the lounge,' she told Dom.

He looked round the rather grand room. It was furnished expensively with a number of rather good antiques. Small tables held china vases which looked Chinese in origin and there was a pretty bureau with a matching tapestry covered stool.

Several pictures hung on the wall, traditional scenes that might have graced any good gallery. Deep leather armchairs, softened with age, were spread around the central area. Lissa indicated one of them. He hesitated, wondering if he sat on the larger sofa, whether she would sit by him.

Lissa, too, was wondering what she should do. If she indicated the sofa, it might look as if she was being somewhat presumptuous. In her heart, she remained convinced that Dom truly cared but he had to tell her himself that he did.

Her father's warnings seemed to be ringing in her ears constantly. She kept telling herself that Dom would never have followed her if he was only after her fortune. He must have wanted to see her . . . really wanted to see her.

She smoothed her cotton shirt over trim fitting trousers. She pushed an imaginary piece of hair from her forehead.

'I hope you had a good flight,' she said nervously.

'Not bad, considering. Look, Lissa, I really need to talk to you. It strikes me that we've been going around in circles ever since we met. It's time we brought everything into the open.'

'OK. If that's what you think. Let's really talk. No more secrets. No fibs.'

Bates knocked at the door and brought in the drinks and a plate of Mrs Bates's own special biscuits.

'I'll be out in the hall, Miss. I'm going to polish the silver. If you need me, you only have to call.'

'Thanks, Bates, but there's no need. I'm fine.'

With a slight inclination of his grey head, he withdrew, still glaring suspiciously at Dom.

'Let's get on with this bout of honesty, shall we?' Dom said firmly.

Surprising News
From Alistair

Why did you want to come to work for me, as a housekeeper, first of all?'

'I told you, my father and I had a row. He said I didn't know anything about working. I didn't even know how to work. I wanted to prove that even he could be wrong for once. I decided the only thing I was any good at was cooking. It was pure coincidence that you happened to be needing someone, just when I went into the agency.'

'I did wonder if you had found out that I needed help and had yourself, set the whole thing up.'

'But I told you, it was all pure luck. Chance happenings. Besides, why on earth would I do that? Set it up, I mean?' Her eyes opened wide as she stared at him in amazement.

'Well, I had no idea of who you were at the time and I'm thought of as quite an eligible bachelor. Something of a catch, despite what you may think.'

'I don't doubt it.'

'For heaven's sake, Lissa. I'm not fooling. I'm not after your money. I've truly got plenty of my own. Please come back to me, Lissa. I don't care what your father threatened. If he disowns you, disinherits you even, I don't care one iota. I can still give you the sort of life you're used to.' He rose from his seat and came over to her.

He put his hand on her shoulder and then moved it to her chin, lifting her mouth towards his. She allowed his lips to brush against her own and instantly felt her heart soaring. He pulled her towards him and set a tiny, gentle kiss on her lips.

Knowing she wasn't pushing him away in any sense, he pulled her to her feet and wrapped her in his arms. Her every doubt, crumbled away. Whatever the circumstances, this was where she was meant to be.

There was a knock at the door and Bates came in.

'I wondered if you'd finished with the coffee cups?' he asked feebly, his voice trailing away as he saw Lissa and Dom deeply entwined in each other's arms.

'Not yet,' Lissa managed to say, struggling to free herself.

'I take everything is in order, Miss?' he asked doubtfully.

'Very much so, thank you,' she said, giving up the struggle to remove Dom's arms. Happily she settled back into the strong, comforting circle. Neither of them heard Bates leave with a discreet cough. She gave a contented sigh.

'Oh, darling Lissa. You've made me so happy. I love you so much.'

'You do? Really?' she was delighted by his words.

'Of course I do. Really. But you must have known that, surely?'

'I thought it but you hadn't ever actually said it to me. Now you have,

I'm certain everything is going to be wonderful.'

'There's so much to discuss. But now I need to go back to Templars. Will you come with me?'

'Of course I will. We're going to Dom's house,' she called out happily to Bates as she was whisked out of the door.

'Are you sure that's what you want?' Bates said to the air behind the vanishing couple. 'I don't know what your father would have to say about that. Oh well, I suppose it will be all right in the end.'

All the same, he wiped away a small, sentimental tear from the corner of his eye. His little Lissa was indeed grown up now.

He went through to the kitchen to break the news to his wife.

'Just the two of us for lunch,' he told her.

'I'm glad. She needs to settle down with someone nice. He does seem a nice boy, doesn't he?'

'I reckon he'll do,' Bates replied. 'He seems to care for her, if what I'm seeing is anything to go by.'

★ ★ ★

'Tell me about your trip,' Dom asked as they drove to his house.

'The usual thing with my father. One posh hotel to the next. Shopping. Sight-seeing. Oh, and I got sick. Some nasty bug. I was in hospital for a while. Couldn't wait to get out and once I was, I couldn't wait to get back. Poor Daddy . . . he was still waiting to see some business clients and I couldn't stand another day. I didn't even say goodbye. Besides, I wanted to see you again and to see if it had really been all a dream.'

'No dream. He did say he had no idea where you were. Tried to tell me you'd left with some other man in tow. I didn't believe for one minute he'd let you leave with anyone he didn't know. No wonder I couldn't find you. And what was wrong with you? Why were you in hospital? Are you certain you're truly better again?'

'Yes, I'm fine again. They thought it was some sort of food poisoning or a bug.'

'I thought you were looking thinner. Are you sure you're all right?'

She nodded.

'Shame we didn't meet up there. It would have saved me a deal of anguish trying to track you down. I'd have so much enjoyed looking around the sights with you. It would have been fun. We could have shopped madly and had tons of excess baggage to pay for.' He was laughing as he spoke.

'But that trip did make me realise how privileged I am. Always have been. Do you know how little money most people earn? I was staggered to see how small my cheque was for working for you for all those weeks.'

'Oh, you're saying I'm mean, am I?'

'Of course not. I didn't mean that. But if that's the sort of money people earn, I don't know how they can afford anything. And in places like the Far East, they seem to work for so little. The ordinary people must have very difficult lives. I feel so guilty when I think about it all.'

'You shouldn't. If it weren't for people like your father and me, for that matter, there would be even more people unemployed. Forget it all for now, Lissa. Let's concentrate on us.' He pulled into the driveway and leapt out of the car. He rushed round to Lissa's side and opened the door. 'Welcome home, my darling.'

'Isn't Mrs Rowley here? Or Jane?' she asked as he pulled her into another hug. He kissed the tip of her nose.

'They are both here. Hoping to welcome you back.'

Jane greeted Lissa like a long lost friend. She hugged her and said how much she'd missed her. Did this mean she was coming back to work? she wanted to know.

'I'm not really sure. Things have

changed,' she told the girl.

'I can see that,' she said, somewhat shyly. 'Do you want anything?' Jane asked as if remembering her own role.

'We could do with a sandwich or something,' Dom said. His body clock was still completely out of sync and he felt ravenous. Lissa raised an eyebrow, teasingly.

'Right. Shall I make it then?' she asked, looking at Lissa for a lead.

'Thanks. That would be good. We'll be in the library. There's a lot we need to talk about.' He took Lissa'a hand and led her in among the pile of books. Nothing had been moved since she was last here. Dom shut the heavy door behind them and pulled her close once more.

'Oh, my love,' he whispered. He pushed her away gently, just in time for Jane's arrival with their lunch snack.

'Afraid there isn't very much food in. I've done cheese. Hope that's OK. I'll have to organise some shopping, if you let me know your plans.'

'Thanks, Jane. That would be excellent,' Dom said calmly. Lissa wished her own response could sound so casual. 'Go on, eat. I insist,' he ordered. 'You need to build up your strength. You do look rather pale and as I say, you've lost weight.'

They shared the simple food and both felt better for it. Lissa was beginning to get back her appetite and Dom's jet lag was fading fast. They talked solidly all afternoon, making plans, changing plans and then talking some more. She noticed a tiny bottle on the side table.

'What's that? It looks like my perfume bottle.'

'I'm sorry,' he said. 'I saw it in your room after you left. You went in something of a hurry and left a lot of things behind you. I used to keep smelling the perfume to remind me of you. I would have bought you some more, but I couldn't find anything exactly like it,' Lissa felt touched.

'That's one of the nicest things I ever

heard.' She wiped away a small amount of moisture that was gathering around her eyes. 'But you wouldn't ever find any more like that one. It's my own blend. My father got it designed for me. Unique and ridiculously expensive, as you might guess. I guess if I worked for you for about six months, it would buy just a few drops.'

'I should have guessed that a housekeeper could not have afforded something that smelled that good. You're going to be one expensive wife to keep.'

'Not necessarily. I've already begun to change. Now I know how hard people have to work, I'm going to change.'

Jane came in with more sandwiches and some tea.

'Don't know if you wanted any more, but I found some canned fish in the cupboard.' She looked shy and awkward as she set down the tray. 'I'll be off now, if that's all right with you, Mr Dom. Lissa.'

'Thanks very much, Jane,' Dom said happily. 'You can be the first to know, Jane. Lissa and I are getting married soon. Very soon.'

'Oh, that's wonderful. Really wonderful. I'm happy for you. When will it be?'

'As soon as we can organise it. Buy yourself something nice to wear. It won't be a long wait.'

Lissa was watching him eating his sandwiches as if he was near starving. She poured the tea and sipped it, fascinated by Dom's appetite.

'If you spend most of your life sitting at a computer, how do you keep so trim?'

'I work out. Haven't you even discovered my gym?'

'What, here? No. In fact, I don't think I've even been into some of the rooms. Mrs Rowley looked after the cleaning and Jane did other things. There was never any need.'

'Then I insist on giving you the grand tour.'

'Actually, if you don't mind I'd like

to leave the tour till later. I need to go back home and I really should call Daddy. He'll be worried.'

'I don't want you to be anywhere other than by my side. Why don't you move here permanently? As my wife? So, how are you fixed for Friday?'

'What are you talking about?'

'The wedding. Can we get married on Friday?'

'We can't possibly. Not a chance. There are too many things to arrange. There's the reception. Guests. Church. A wedding dress. Flowers. Bridesmaids. Daddy is still in Hong Kong anyhow. Besides. Don't you have to have licences and things?'

'OK. I'll give you till Monday. I'll sort the licence. You can get a special licence that is valid in just a few days. And you can invite whoever you think should come. You don't want some big fancy affair, do you?'

'I don't know,' she muttered. None of this was going to plan. Not her plan anyhow. 'I suppose I don't want a big wedding but it must be a special day. We shall have to invite a few people. Jane and Mrs Rowley from your side. And Bates and Mrs Bates from my side. They'd never forgive me if they didn't see me properly married.'

'OK. So we have a slightly larger affair than just the two of us. Do you think your father will come?'

'I'm sure he will. I don't think he actually disliked you.'

'Not the impression I got when I met up with him. He sent me packing with a never darken my doorstep again attitude.'

'He'll come round.'

'Right. That's the wedding sorted. Now about the honeymoon. I thought we'd take six months, no, nine months to travel. Do all the things we've ever wanted to do. I can easily keep up with the office through emails. We'll have such a wonderful time.

'Think of what we can do. We'll enjoy life so much, my darling. I promise you. Just you and I, together. It will be wonderful. Where shall we go first? I fancy South America. We can stroll through Macchu Pichu. Fly over the Andes. Go to Rio for the Carnival. What do you say?'

'It sounds wonderful, of course. And I really do want a family. I want to give our children the sort of life you and I both missed out. Besides, this is a family home. It cries out for a large, noisy gang of children rushing everywhere.'

'There's time for all this later. Let's go back to Ingleton. You can call your father with the news and tell your Mr and Mrs Bates.'

'Get Bates and Mrs Bates onside and we're home and dry, Daddy listens to them about anything concerning me. If they approve of you, we're OK. We'll go and have a drink and a chat with them. Champagne's called for, I think.'

They arrived at Ingleton Manor.

'Bates? Mrs Bates? Are you there?' The elderly couple came through from the kitchen looking slightly anxious.

'Good news. Have we got some cold Champagne? We're celebrating. Come into the lounge with it when you've found it.' She breezed into the pretty room and dragged Dom after her.

'For all your talk of not wanting to be rich, you have a very long way to go. You're still giving your orders.'

'Old habits.'

A few minutes later, Bates came in with a tray loaded with a bottle and two glasses. 'We need two more glasses,' she told him. 'And Mrs Bates is wanted too.'

Dom picked up the bottle and took off the foil and wire and popped the cork just as the couple came in. He took the extra glasses and poured out the drinks.

'We're getting married, dear Bates and Mrs Bates. Isn't it wonderful? Aren't you going to drink to our health?'

'Of course, Miss. We're happy for you both, but does your father know? He won't be pleased if you haven't told him.'

'He sort of knows. I'm going to phone him in a while and give him the good news. He has met Dom, so he won't be too surprised.'

'Then good luck to you both. When do you think the wedding will be?'

'As soon as possible. We won't have a big wedding. Nothing grand. Just a simple affair. Next week if Lissa can manage it.' Dom was in full flow.

'Don't be so silly. It will be weeks before you can get a dress designed and made and the reception will all need organising and the church and besides, your father's still away. Oh, and the cake needs a minimum of three months soaking before it's even iced. Oh dear, such a lot to be done. But we shall do it, I'm sure. Oh how exciting.' Mrs Bates was already making mental lists and her grin was spreading across her face.

'Don't get too excited about all of that, Mrs B. I really don't intend to have a big wedding.'

'But your father will never allow it. He will want the full works with all his friends and colleagues present. It will be the talk of the county for months.' Her face was woebegone and tears were filling her eyes.

'You know what? I'd really like one of your giant chocolate cakes for a wedding cake. The way you can make it at the last minute and if we do get organised for next week, there's still plenty of time.'

'Oh, dear me. It really won't do at all. But you know your own mind, I suppose. Let's see what your father says when you talk to him. Now, I need to get back to the kitchen. Will you be staying for dinner, Mr Dominic?'

'I suppose I could, if it's all right with you. Be nice to see Lissa's home and get a bit closer view of her life. Now, can I top your glass up?'

'We'll leave you youngsters alone,' Bates said as they left.

'What a lovely couple. No wonder you're so fond of them. What do you think they'll do once you've left home?'

'I'd like to think they'll retire. I'm

hoping to persuade Daddy to buy them a little cottage nearby. They've been everything to me. Better than parents in a way.' She finished her drink and put the glasses on the tray.

It was a pleasant evening, making plans and talking of their life together, as they ate one of Mrs Bates delicious meals.

'Did you ever get in touch with your father?' Dom asked.

'No. The time was wrong. I'll try now though, if that's OK?'

'I'd like to be here to hear what he says,' Dom replied. 'Well, I think I should be in case there are problems. I can pick up the pieces.'

She glared at him as she dialled his mobile number. A female voice answered.

'I'm sorry if I disturbed you. I was trying to speak to Alistair Langham. I must have the wrong number.'

'No. This is right. He's in a meeting. I'll call him.'

Lissa put her hand over the phone and spoke to Dom. 'He's in a meeting, apparently. Some woman answered. English accent. Hello? Daddy? Who on earth was that answering your phone?' She paused, listening.

Dom felt frustrated as he heard one side of the conversation, especially when it didn't seem to be with reference to their own plans.

'Daddy, listen. I'm pleased you have a companion, but I do think I deserve the truth for once. No, I'm fine. Yes. Thank you.'

She paused again to listen and went pale. She sat down heavily as she listened to something her father was telling her. Dom watched anxiously.

'I see,' she continued. 'No. It's a bit of a shock but then life is rather full of shocks, isn't it? No, I'm all right. Really. But now, I need you to listen to me. I have some news of my own. Dom and I are getting married. As soon as possible. Yes, that's right. Next week if we can organise it. When are you coming back? We might be able to wait for a couple of weeks . . . yes, I know.'

At last it seemed the conversation was coming to an end.

'Yes. Of course you can bring her. How long has it been? Good lord. Why on earth didn't you tell me before? Yes. Goodbye.'

She put the phone down.

'So, what on earth was all that about? I gather he didn't try to forbid any of our plans?'

'I've just learned that my father has fallen in love. Can you believe it? I still wonder why he didn't tell me. It must have been when I was away early last year. Why keep it such a secret?'

'And what did he say about us?' Dom asked patiently.

'He didn't say much. They'll try to be back for the wedding providing it isn't too soon.'

'If that's what you want,' Dom said. 'I was hoping we wouldn't have to wait too long.'

'I'm sorry, Dom, but I really do need a few minutes to let this sink in. All these months Daddy has been trying to control my life and he's been with someone. I wouldn't have minded.'

'Look, I can understand you are feeling shocked, but we still have such a lot to discuss ourselves.'

'You know, I still feel a bit weak and very tired. It's been quite a day. I can't believe it was only this morning that you came over. Can we spend tomorrow discussing things?'

'Good idea. In fact, I'm suddenly feeling exhausted myself. The jet lag is finally catching up on me, not to mention the excitement and drama of a life with you around. I hope you can manage to get a proper sleep tonight. I'm very excited by it all and more relieved than I can say.'

'And happy? Most of all, happy?'

'Certainly that. I can never remember being so happy. But I'll leave you now. Come over to Templars tomorrow?'

'If you like.'

'Hey, I never did give you the tour of the house.'

'Tomorrow.'

'I've Got You Now'

Shouldn't I be actually doing something about the wedding?' he asked when she arrived at his home the next morning. 'Sort out licences or whatever's needed?'

'Find out about it, I'd say. Don't commit to anything though. Not until we know what's going to happen.'

'You do want us to get married, don't you?'

'Of course I do, Dom. I'm not sure how my father's going to be about it all though.'

'You should stop relying on your father quite so much. No disrespect, but he does seem to dominate everything you want to do.'

'My father has been wonderful to me, all my life. Generous. Everything I always wanted.'

'Always? Everything?'

'Well, he was always very busy so he didn't always have enough time to do everything I wanted. I suppose it was his time and company I wanted. But, that's all in the past. I've got you now.'

They spent the day relaxing around the house and planning some changes to the décor. Without a firm date, they could do nothing more about the wedding, despite the huge amount of organising they were going to need for the extended honeymoon once the ceremony was over. After two days, Dom had had enough.

'Exactly when are your father and his friend returning?'

'They're not sure. Maybe next week.'

'Right. We are setting the date for our wedding, be they here or not. Agreed?'

'Agreed.'

'Friday week. That will be the beginning of June. It's a good time.'

'Fine.'

If Dom wanted to organise everything, she was quite happy to go along with him. The only thing that mattered to her, was that they should get married.

He had reached the final list of guests stage when he realised she was simply not listening.

'Darling, what's wrong?'

'Absolutely nothing. I was just thinking how lucky I am. I'm about to marry the man I love.'

'You don't care who comes to the wedding, do you?'

'As long as you and I are there, that's all that matters. But we do need to invite Bates and Mrs Bates.'

'And Jane. And Mrs Rowley. And we can hardly leave Harris out, can we?'

'And maybe Lettie Jenkins should come too. After all, if it hadn't been for her . . .'

Dom laughed. 'I'll get on to it straight away,' he said. 'And then I'll book the first stage of our honeymoon. You might need to do some shopping. I doubt you've got everything you might need, even in that massive closet of yours.'

'What about the reception? Even for so few guests, we need to do something.'

'I'll phone Lettie Jenkins and see if she can recommend someone,' he said with a laugh.

'I must go and find a wedding dress.'

Lissa spent a hectic few days shopping and planning, punctuated by numerous phone calls to Dom, who was equally busy organising his work so it could be left for several months.

They heard nothing from her father and had almost given up any hope that he would be present.

Despite being one of the honoured guests, Mrs Bates had insisted that the wedding reception should take place at Ingleton Manor. She would hear of nothing else and her one concession to the extra work, was to take on someone to help in the kitchen with preparations and someone to serve on the day itself.

She had contacted a local florist to come and decorate the house and by the Thursday evening before the big day, the entire house was looking magnificent.

Heavy cream roses spilled out of large pots in each of the main rooms and a magnificent arrangement of green and cream flowers and leaves adorned the hallway. As Lissa came in from her final shopping trip, she gasped in delight.

'Mrs Bates, you've done wonders. It all looks simply amazing. Thank you so much. You see, it didn't take so very long to bring it all together. Now, let's have a cup of tea and I'll help with any last minute things that need doing in the kitchen.'

'Of course you won't.'

'But I'd love to. After all, it was my cooking skills that brought Dom and me together in the first place.'

★ ★ ★

The whole party had assembled at Ingleton Manor by ten o'clock the next morning when Lissa saw a car pull up outside.

'Who on earth is that?' Dom asked, a trifle cross that his plans may be interrupted.

'It's Daddy. And I think there's someone with him.' She got out of the car, watching, nervous and slightly anxious. Surely he couldn't stop anything at this late stage? She stepped forward.

'Are we in time, darling?' asked Alistair, as he rushed over to her. He put his arms round her and held her close. 'Darling girl. I want you to be happy. I hope you are?'

'Yes, Daddy. I'm very happy. I'm so glad you got here in time.'

'No formal wedding dress?'

'No. I'm a simple soul at heart.' Lissa had decided on a simple cream silk dress with a long straight skirt and a plain, fitted top. She wore a tiny ring of fresh flowers tucked into her hair which was knotted on top of her head, the way Dom liked it best.

'You look perfect. But then you always do. Is there time for you to meet my friend, Amanda, before the service? She is longing to meet you.'

Hesitantly, Alistair's companion climbed out of the car. The two women approached each other, hands outstretched.

'Hello, Lissa. I'm so pleased to meet you at last.'

'Hello, Amanda.' Lissa stopped, staring at the rather homely woman.

'I don't know what to say,' Alistair finally gathered himself together and stammered. 'I don't suppose there is much I can say except congratulations to you.'

'I'm so happy you're here Daddy and Amanda, of course.'

'You made your own choice in the end, Melissa. All by yourself. I love you and I'm very proud of you.'

Dom and Lissa were married in the grounds of Ingleton Manor in a simple ceremony while her beloved father looked on. It was time for a new beginning.

We do hope that you have enjoyed reading this large print book.

Did you know that all of our titles are available for purchase?

We publish a wide range of high quality large print books including:
Romances, Mysteries, Classics
General Fiction
Non Fiction and Westerns

Special interest titles available in large print are:
The Little Oxford Dictionary
Music Book, Song Book
Hymn Book, Service Book

Also available from us courtesy of Oxford University Press:
Young Readers' Dictionary
(large print edition)
Young Readers' Thesaurus
(large print edition)

For further information or a free brochure, please contact us at:
Ulverscroft Large Print Books Ltd.,
The Green, Bradgate Road, Anstey,
Leicester, LE7 7FU, England.
Tel: (00 44) **0116 236 4325**
Fax: (00 44) **0116 234 0205**

LADY CHARLOTTE'S SECRET

Fenella Miller

Determined to fulfil her promise to a friend, Charlotte defies her brother and sets out on a journey in secret. But the person most at risk is herself, as circumstances conspire to leave her helpless in the care of a stranger. Dr James Hunter is a modern man, dedicating his life to aristocracy. When he discovers Charlotte's secret will it destroy their love?

SNOWBOUND

Fay Cunningham

When Amy agrees to help famous cosmetic surgeon Ethan Stopes write his memoirs, she is expecting a few quiet days in the country. Instead she spends an eventful Christmas trapped in a lonely manor with Ethan, his ex-wife, and his two children — and falls in love . . . Amy discovers Ethan's secret, and passions flare as the snow deepens. Somehow, she must help the enigmatic surgeon finish his book before it is too late . . .